A HOLLY JOLLY REAPER

A Grim Reaper Holiday Adventure

Riya Aarini

A Holly Jolly Reaper: A Grim Reaper Holiday Adventure

ISBN: 978-1-956496-53-6 (Paperback)

ISBN: 978-1-956496-54-3 (eBook)

www.riyapresents.com

The spicy cardamom and vanilla scents wafted over my face bones as I pulled open the front door to headquarters—ah, gingerbread. It was a welcome aroma, one I hadn't sniffed in exactly a year. It simply meant I was soon in for a freshly baked treat or two of ginger and molasses.

I scuffled out of the frigid cold and hurried into the warmth of the building. With a wiggle, I shook the newly fallen snow off my tattered black cloak and wiped my damp feet bones on the coir doormat that read *Welcome to Afterlife HQ. Hope You Stay a While.*

As I grasped the rail on my way up the spiral staircase, the needles of the pine garland and the twigs of the red berry sprigs poked me in the hand bones. I had a mind to swat at them to avoid the painful sensations. More was definitely *more* when it came to decorating, and less was appreciated for the sake of safety.

Halfway up the stairs, I picked up the high-spirited tune of "Frosty the Snowman" playing through the ceiling speakers. My facial features tightened. It was a staggering feat of either simplicity or ingenuity that a songwriter came up with a silk hat that could bring to life three snowballs. Frosty may have been a jolly, happy soul, but I didn't feel compelled to be one in the slightest.

Biting the inside of my cheekbone, I made my way into the office.

"Reaper!" Life cried out. Stunning as ever in her body-hugging red velvet dress, she teetered on a stepstool, hanging little elf paper cutouts with smiling faces of the afterlife staff. "Do you mind?" she asked pointing to one of the elves lying flat on the carpeted floor as if it had just croaked.

"Um, certainly." I bent down, picked it up, and handed it to her. "You do have a knack for decorating."

"It's one of my favorite times of the year."

As she hummed and lightly tapped her foot to the holiday music, her merriment was clear.

"Humph," was all I could muster in return.

My gaze wandered to the red stockings, hung neatly in a row with their toes pointed to the left. I'd long known about the unsolvable quandary of whether to point the stocking toes to the left or to the right. As a phantasm who found little joy in stocking stuffers in the first place, I yawned and gave it no more thought.

"Help yourself to some gingerbread cookies," Life said. "I baked them early this morning."

"Sounds delish."

I sauntered toward the food table. With a hand bone full of cookies shaped like mischievously grinning, balding souls, I passed Death's door, now covered in ruby-red wrapping paper with a giant metallic gold bow across the center. It was slightly ajar, so I poked my skull in.

"Hey, boss."

"Reaper, care for a sip?"

Death held up a tall, slender bottle of eggnog. The label was red-and-white, with Old English lettering.

My skeleton perked up. The smoky whiff of brandy wafting from the bottle drew me into his office like a south pole magnet attracted a north pole one.

"Don't mind if I do." I shimmied over next to his desk.

Death poured me a glass of spiked eggnog, which he served warm—the perfect welcome after coming in from the blustery cold. I guzzled the delicious drink in seconds.

"Gets us into the festive mood, eh?" He winked.

"No doubt, boss. Nothing's sweeter than a rich eggnog splashed with an even more satisfying Cognac."

I smacked my jawbone and expressed my appreciation for his generosity.

Thanks to this strong drink first thing in the morning, I strolled to my cubicle with a pep in my step. Along the way, I passed several cubicles decorated as snowy fairytale gingerbread houses or cozy fireplaces complete with red-brick chimneys.

I tilted my skeleton toward the structures, wondering how the holidays drove the afterlife staff to exert such monumental decorative effort. Indeed, there must've been some magic involved in the most magical time of year.

My curiosity was fleeting, as one of them called out: "Hey, Reaper!"

It was Larry, the spirit guide. I stopped over at his desk, which gave me the feeling of having just been invited into his family room. The image of a roaring fireplace graced his computer screen. Red stockings hung from his cubicle walls, and green Santa directional signs to the North Pole lay plastered along the sides.

He offered me a classic peppermint candy cane.

"Um, no thanks. I'm trying to watch my figure." Truthfully, the last thing I needed was a foul aftertaste and sticky hand bones.

"Any plans for the holidays?" he asked, biting off the curled end off with an idle *snap*.

"Who, me?" My shoulder bones curled over my rib cage.

"Yeah, you. I'm spending the holidays with my extended family. They're coming over from all corners of eternity. We'll be baking a ham and making candied sweet potatoes, then opening presents and sipping hot cocoa all day long.

It'll be the most meaningful together time of the year."

I frowned and gazed down at my pigeon toe bones.

"Nah, it'll be just me and my scythe," I blurted out in monosyllabic tones. "I'll be pretty busy. Maybe I'll volunteer to work extra shifts on the twenty-fifth."

With my chin bone lowered to my rib cage, I plodded toward my cubicle. On my way, I passed by desks covered with holiday-themed wooden frames showcasing photos of happy staff members wearing Santa hats, their arms wrapped snug around loved ones, holiday greeting cards pinned to their cork boards, and signs suggesting the importance of togetherness around the holiday tree.

As I stumbled toward my desk, employees of all levels wished me happy holidays with genuine smiles. I recoiled, but managed a low grunt in response to each of them.

Finally, I made it to my cubicle, plain as jane, and ducked into it before anyone else could wish me a happy holiday season or gloat about their joyful togetherness.

I shuffled a mess of papers as the joy of Christmas went over my skull. It was, however, the perfect holiday to highlight my unbearable loneliness. Death reveled in the company of Life, and they remained endlessly intertwined like sultry tango dancers in a wild embrace. All the spirit guides' friends and family stayed in their locality for eternity, right where the guides were stationed—in the glorious afterlife, brimming with unconditional love and healing light. But me, lowly, lonely me, had not one fond companion in the between-realm of the living and the dead. I remained despicably, pathetically alone. Forever.

Another spirit guide floated past, dressed in ethereal white. "Happy holidays, Reaper!" she greeted with an annoyingly sincere smile.

I wrinkled my nasal cavity and disappeared behind the pile of papers until she passed. Ugh, the pressure was on to love a holiday that everyone loved—except me.

Andy Williams's soul crooned "It's the Most Wonderful Time of Year" from the speakers. He'd sung it nine minutes ago—yet still hadn't convinced me it was anywhere close to being the most wonderful time of year. Following it, "Let it Snow" played, then Bing Crosby's "Frosty the Snowman" again. I was forced to listen to the same nauseating twelve songs, on repeat, over and over again until my mind went numb.

Cassandra, another spirit guide, whizzed past my desk. "Ready for the white elephant gift exchange tomorrow?"

My skeleton shot up. I'd forgotten I needed to bring in a little something. "Ready as I'll ever be!" I fibbed, giving her a nervous thousand-watt smile.

"Great! It'll be a whole lot of fun, just like the entire holiday season. Bring something everyone will want to steal. The price range is $10 to $25." With a hop and skip, she pranced like Santa's reindeer toward the copy machine at the other end of the office.

I sank in my chair. Ten to twenty-five dollars? I dug into my empty cloak pockets and turned them inside out. Payday wasn't for eons, leaving me staring out into nothingness. The white elephant holiday gift exchange was another stark reminder of how broke a reaper I was.

With the mounting pressure to be jolly, the impossible focus on togetherness, and the unreasonable expectation to spend lavishly, I wanted to flash forward to January pronto.

I sat at my desk, making myself small and contemplating that, if Christmas returned to its pagan roots, it'd be worth celebrating. Maybe with a heaping bowl of psychedelic Amanita muscaria mushrooms, with the festive red-and-white spots. Ah, now *that* was a scintillating holiday treat!

In the meantime, I had to find something quick for the white elephant gift exchange.

The end of the workday approached. Per the rules of the game, I wouldn't leave tomorrow's gift exchange empty handed. Maybe by some random fluke of the universe, I'd get the present I'd fancied for ages: a cocktail smoker kit with a torch to smoke my own cocktails. The mere thought sent tingles down my spine.

All it took was one unforgettable gift from someone to show me I was appreciated—and receiving a cocktail smoker kit didn't require me to feign a look of amazement or gratitude. It'd truly be the best gift ever.

On my way to the store, I stopped at the bar and ordered a shot. Thank goodness for vodka. Clear, smooth, one-hundred proof. I could drink it straight to get me through Christmas.

Bah humbug.

The afterlife staff gathered in the conference room, eager to participate in this year's white elephant gift exchange. A teetering mountain of presents sat atop the banquet-size table. None of us saw which staff members had hand-wrapped and dropped off the gifts. They were all anonymous.

I looked around the exquisitely decorated conference hall, admiring the ice palace theme. Blue glacial lights shone from the ceiling in a vibe of Arctic, otherworldly comfort. White pompoms in the shape of ten-pointed snowflakes hung from above. The backs of our chairs featured illustrations of gnomes dressed up in slouching winter hats.

The jovial atmosphere sent a lightness through my skeleton. Maybe this Christmas would be different. I smoothed out the wrinkles in my cloak, feeling worthy of change in the right direction.

Moe, a spirit guide, grabbed a seat on the opposite side of the circle with Larry, Cassandra, and several other spirit guides. Most of the staff consisted of dedicated spirit guides, as they were integral to the next world. Kind of like gregarious tour guides taking newcomers through a strange, new place.

Dressed in a black polo shirt and with his muscular arms crossed over his massive chest, Death stood near the entrance, next to gorgeous Life. She looked striking in her belted velvet green dress. Sounding chipper as ringing bells, they chatted as the rest of the afterlife team sauntered in.

Minutes before the game began, the Cosmic Light made his grand entrance. A brilliant, whitish glow surrounded his majestic, looming figure. He was the head honcho, the ultimate Creator of all of existence, superior even to Life and Death. In fact, they answered to him–the magnanimous force that held the cardinal power in the known and unknown universe.

My bones trembled at his sheer, sweeping authority.

Smiling politely, the Cosmic Light exchanged a few pleasantries with Death and Life and, crossing one mighty leg over the other, nestled into a seat in the circle with the rest of the afterlife staff.

Being low in the office hierarchy, I rarely spoke to the Cosmic Light. The one time I had didn't go very well: "Heya, Cosmic Light. How's it feel to be the kingpin, the big dog, the captain of all existence?" I'd yammered. "Everything that goes wrong in the universe is your fault!"

I'd slapped my hand bone against my knee bone, but I was the only one laughing.

I'd tried again: "Managing all of existence is like managing a cemetery. You've got a lot of folks under you, but they're busy doing nothing!"

The Cosmic Light had spent no more than a nanosecond glancing at me with a confused expression before marching off—and still not cracking a smile. We'd never exchanged more than two words since. The universe's supreme power ought to have a better sense of humor.

I settled in amongst the circle of chairs. The seat next to me remained empty, but with at least four hundred afterlife staff expected at the white elephant gift exchange, it ought to be filled soon. Before I even finished my thought, Joey, one of the many winged cherubs, plopped down next to me.

He gave me a childlike smile, which I returned with an ominous grin. With his rosy cheeks and curly blond locks, he radiated pure innocence. Clearly trying to get comfortable, the cherub flapped his white wings. His feathers brushed against my skeleton, tickling me to no end.

I began hooting and hollering, angling my skeleton away from the source of the tickle. Amid my uncontrollable laughter, I turned to him and pointed at his flapping feathers.

"Oh, sorry, Reaper," he replied with a soft, charming apologetic tone.

The redness left my face bones.

Joey settled down and brought his wings close to his pudgy little figure. I let out a huge breath, not expecting to suffer another tickle for the rest of the event.

As holiday tunes played, Life, in all her glory, strutted into the center of the circle.

I bounced my knee bones. The games were about to begin.

"Valued afterlife staff, may I have your attention please?" Life said.

The team members quieted down, and they stopped their rambunctious fidgeting.

"Today is our spectacular white elephant holiday gift exchange," Life announced. "Death and I are pleased you've come from all corners of eternity to participate in this event."

I drummed my feet bones on the carpet as she reached down and grabbed an ornate golden bowl, shining bright as a star. "You'll each pick a number, which will determine the order you'll choose a gift."

Life approached me with the glistening golden orb in hand. "Reaper, pick a number."

Meeting her warm gaze, I dug my finger bones into the bowl overflowing with papers. I picked out a white cutout elephant with a number on it. My jaw pressed into a tight grimace. "Ugh, I got number one." A low number meant I had the least number of chances to steal potentially fantastic gifts.

Frank, one of the cherubs seated a few seats down, snickered.

Ignoring him, I plodded toward the gift table with a hunched posture. The pile of presents reached an inch away from the ceiling. I eyed the boxes wrapped in shimmery paper, wishing I had x-ray vision to see what was inside each of them. But I didn't, so I simply chose the biggest gift on the table.

With sweaty hand bones, I began unwrapping the box measuring ten square feet, the size of half a bed. It took a while, but here in the afterlife, white elephant gift exchanges could literally go on for eternity.

On tearing off the last bit of wrapping paper, I came across another, slightly smaller box inside the first large box. I scratched my cheekbone. Hmm, the presentation was inventive.

My colleagues started shifting in their seats. I hurried up, only to find another box inside the second box–then the third, and so on, till I reached a box the size of a jewelry case.

The impressive gift box I'd originally started with ended up as a measly box in the palm of my hand bone. I winced.

"Open it!" someone shouted.

I undid the ribbon and opened the diminutive box, only to pull out a slip of paper. It was a lottery ticket with the words *Win up to $250,000 cash!* emblazoned across it in neon letters.

“Scratch it!” another colleague yelled.

I glanced around the room, somewhat frustrated that my humungous gift was reduced to a slip of paper. Who could’ve had the nerve to do suck a trick?

Then the whole room chanted, “Scratch, scratch, scratch!”

My chest cavity pounded. My attention remained laser-focused on the paper.

Maybe this holiday would be my luckiest yet. No longer would I be a broke reaper. Two-hundred-and-fifty-thousand dollars richer and highly respected, I’d waltz through the office in a brand-new cloak, a blinged-out scythe, and a thick, gold chain around my neck bones. I fanned myself with the ticket that determined my fate. Holding my breath, I scratched off the foil with my pinky bone.

My arm bones went limp. None of the numbers matched. I’d received a dud gift.

I stomped to my seat and plonked down with a heavy sigh. My gift wasn’t steal-worthy, and no one bothered.

Despite my dashed hopes, the game went on. The colleague who’d picked number two chose her gift— and so on—until everyone had a gift of some sort.

The items ranged from a volume of Christmas carols sung by the local angel choir to a beat-up Viking board game, played in Greenland two thousand years ago.

The Cosmic Light's eyes lit up when he unwrapped a giant pencil. But Larry quickly stole it.

I did a double take when a used garden gnome became a big hit—it'd been stolen three times. Equally eye socket opening was the screaming-goat stress reliever that everyone wanted. Working in the afterlife headquarters could be stressful, which made the bleating goat a highly sought-after trinket.

The cherubs and spirit guides alike clamored to steal a calendar with photos of dogs' faces underwater. It was the most popular gift of the exchange, even among the fifteen days' worth of light-up socks.

Cassandra unwrapped a tortilla blanket with which she could wrap herself up like a burrito inside the chilly office. Life leaped out of her chair, pointed, and exclaimed, "I'm stealing the blanket!" The spirit guide hugged the blanket against her chest, refusing to let go. But the rules of the game prevailed, and Life successfully stole the hot item.

I made the gargantuan effort to steal a coffee mug printed with a photo of Life, my eternal crush, as a college-aged student, her vibrant red hair in two side braids. Everyone else had the same idea. But I clenched my teeth when I failed to get my hand bones on it.

Moe's turn came. The old spirit guide shuffled up to the gift table and selected a rectangular, nine-foot-high gift, wrapped expertly with visually stunning paper. I rubbed my finger bones against my rib cage and blew on them. This gift would be highly coveted, and stolen the most. I could feel it in the depths of my abdominal cavity. I sat motionless and watched, barely breathing.

He tore off the wrapping paper from the top, revealing the corner of a richly hued mahogany frame. He ripped off more paper. The image of a midnight black hood appeared. Once he'd unwrapped the whole thing, my colleagues gasped and turned to stare at me incredulously.

"What?" I sank low in my chair, adding, "It's a life-size picture of yours truly. I'm a gift to the afterworld," to judgmental glares. A flush swept across my face bones. Humph. No one stole it.

After all the laughter, jollity, and condemnatory stares, the event wound down. I left with nothing but a losing lottery ticket and a bitterness filling my rib cage. It was another insufferable instance of how the festive season normally treated me.

I returned to the office after completing the day's rounds, only to be pulled into the ugly sweater station near the entrance. No onsite employee could escape being sucked into an instance of despondent humiliation disguised as holiday cheer. Complicating matters, the crafty holiday crew viewed my plain black cloak as the ultimate canvas.

"We'll glam you up for the holidays," they said gleefully, and scurried for the felt markers.

I didn't need glamming up. No reaper did. It was against the in-between realm policy.

Nevertheless, the staff hauled me into a corner.

My skull recoiled at all the photos of the ugly sweaters worn by prior staffers. They, too, had been lured into wearing these concerningly endearing expressions of merriment. The sweaters ranged from an image of an apple-headed chihuahua donning oversized neon-green sunglasses to a 3D reindeer whose protruding fuzzy antlers served as props for a casual game of ring toss. I grimaced at the photo of the ugly sweatered employee smiling at the stuffed squirrel perched on his shoulder. And yet, despite my instinctual response, it was impossible to look away.

"No, really, it's not necessary," I protested, pushing my hand bones in front of me as they draped a shimmery green garland around my cloak.

"You need to get into the holiday spirit," said one of the staff as she hooked shiny silver ornaments on the garland. "I've never seen anyone so grim this time of year."

I tried to argue, but my words dried up mid-sentence. So I grunted.

A few torturous minutes and a boxload of green garlands later, they insisted I pose for a photo.

"What? For everyone to see?" I exclaimed, stumbling back a step.

"Wait!" cried a colleague. She rushed over to a nearby cardboard box, picked a glittery red bow the size of my scythe blade, and stuck it to my cloak.

The other staff clearly felt inspired, and began pinning tinier sparkly bows on every inch of free cloak space they managed to find. I turned my skull to the side, wishing I could shut my eye sockets.

They stood back to look me over, their chins resting on their hands. "Something's missing."

One of the staff snapped her fingers. "I know!"

She reached over and plucked a string of fairy lights from a box, then proceeded to wrap me in the tangle of green wire and colorful bulbs.

"I can't move my arm bones," I said, as she roped the illuminations around and around my skeleton.

She kissed her fingers with flourish. "Marvelous. The perfect finishing touch. Now you look like a full-skeleton Christmas tree."

I tried to diffuse my horror verbally. "The ugly sweater look isn't my thing. I'd appreciate you unraveling the string of–"

"Smile for the camera!" said another staffer, holding up a tablet.

Before I could complain further, she took my photo: a frowning, restrained reaper wearing the ugliest Christmas cloak ever to be seen.

"I hope that photo's not going on a Christmas card," I muttered and hobbled away.

I reached my desk without being accosted by any more highly spirited colleagues. Breathing a sigh, I sorted through piles of random paperwork.

The speakers blared the same holiday tunes over and over in a tiring loop. Although the music was written to be singable, I didn't even feel like humming their melodies. Rather, listening to the high-frequency sounds of bells clanking, old-fashioned crooning, and uber-cheerful lyrics made my skull spin. An uneasiness grew in the pit of my abdominal cavity.

I attempted to ease my nausea by distracting myself with my full inbox. Maybe reading a few emails would help me tune out the monotonous holiday music.

As I scoured through the emails, my attention went to one with a line of Christmas tree emojis. I squinted and leaned forward.

It was a memo from Life, my eternal crush. I clicked.

Fighting my dizziness, I rapidly scanned the message. Hmm, Life wanted the staff to write letters to Santa.

I scratched my skull. Why would grownups send a letter to Santa, of all mythical characters? He was nothing more than a jolly old man who worked one day a year. I certainly had no respect for him. Humph. I gave my skull a quick shake, trying to make sense of the bizarre memo on my computer screen.

As I battled my lightheadedness and urge to vomit, I flung my perturbations out the window and began typing a letter, per Life's wishes. I couldn't say no to her, the secret love and light of my existence.

But it'd be no ordinary letter, filled with the typical artificial niceties.

Listen, Santa. I'm not going to beat around the Christmas tree. I've never gotten anything good for Christmas. In fact, I've never received anything at all over the past seven hundred years I've been slaving away as the notorious grim reaper. Now, you may think I'm naughty, being grim all year round, but it's a part of my persona—

just like being jolly is a part of yours. You ought to understand. We've both been at our eternal positions for centuries. I'll make this short. All I want for Christmas is a cocktail smoker kit with a torch. It's no fun without the torch, so don't forget it. – Reaper

I hit Print and marched over to the printer.

I snatched the letter, folded it, and slipped it into a beige envelope with a winking reindeer on the front flap and a border of candy canes. Using a felt tip pen, I scribbled Santa's address: *123 Santa Claus Lane, North Pole, 88888.* Santa enjoyed the privilege of having an entire street named after him. I didn't even own a home with an address to call my own. I stayed in cheap rentals. What a gyp!

I clenched my jawbone. I had a mind to rip up the letter and toss it into the wire trash basket. But I refrained in favor of respecting Life's wishes.

With flinty eye sockets, I licked the envelope and sealed it. Writing this letter had fueled my unspoken envy of the legendary man in red.

Nasal cavities flaring, I stomped outside and down to the block corner, where the blue Afterlife Postal Service (ALPS) bin stood bolted to the sidewalk, and dropped it into the slender opening. I heard a light thump at the bottom of the bin. I checked the pickup time—at two o'clock—dry wiped my hand bones, and returned to the office to finish up the day's tasks. All the while wondering why Santa couldn't just accept text or email. I had to go out of my way to send this *elite* figure snail mail.

An ulcer came on as I ruminated about Santa's innumerable fortunes, and my hard luck.

Nevertheless, I busied myself until the four o'clock hour, when I packed up my scythe to go home. Cassandra, wearing her customary dowdy smile, strolled up to my desk as I tucked my blade sharpener away in my desk drawer.

"Hey, Reaper. Did you get the memo?"

"What memo?" I asked. Engulfed by spite, workplace communications had escaped my attention. All I could focus on was how Santa had it good, while I toiled away without a hint of the respect or commendation he so easily garnered.

"You know, the one from Life asking us to write letters from Santa," she said, her annoying smile still plastered on her round face.

Then it hit me like Santa's sled, cruising at seventy miles per hour.

I stared at her speechless for a long minute. "What d'you mean *from* Santa?"

"Life. She wanted us to write letters from Santa to the kids on Earth. It's supposed to be a benevolent gesture to show the afterlife's good spirits toward the children in the Earthly community."

My eye sockets widened. I rolled my shoulder bones and twisted my neck bone.

I'd goofed, making me feel smaller than Santa's elves.

She leaned in, still smiling. "Well?"

I whispered "No!" under my breath, then attempted to explain. "I guess I got the memo, but I-I wasn't feeling well and misread it, thinking it'd asked me to write *to* Santa. I did and asked for what I wanted and posted it." I dropped my skull into my hand bones. "The ALPS already picked up the mail. It's on its way to the North Pole as we speak!"

I clutched my empty mid-section, as my rib cage caved in.

Cassandra's smile never left her face. Holding the unofficial title as the cheeriest of spirit guides, she offered words of solace. "Don't worry. It's just a formality. Plus, Santa will probably never get it, much less read it. The ALPS isn't reliable anyway." She turned and walked away.

I covered my face bones with my hand bones and slowly shook my skull.

Writing a candid letter to my nemesis wasn't the way I intended to start the holiday season.

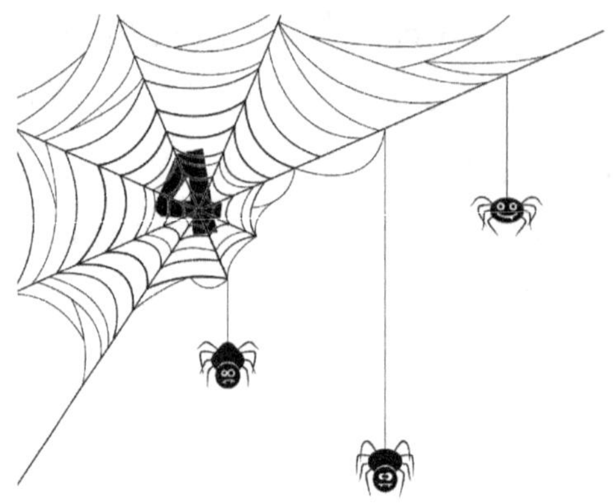

Standing tall, I rowed across the murky river with my last client of the day in tow. He was a glum, thirtyish fellow, who'd been whisked away while untangling string lights on the roof of his two-story house. A strong wind had blown against his wobbly twenty-four-foot ladder, sending him tumbling to the ground. I appeared two seconds later to collect his soul.

As we approached the banks of eternity, I told him he could hang all the string lights he wanted in the next world—and he'd never need to bother with the hassle of replacing burnt-out bulbs. But he might not need to deal with lights at all, unless he wanted to, because it was the land of eternal light. His face upturned slightly as I mentioned the pluses of the afterworld.

I helped him off the boat and wished him a happy stay.

Pushing through the frigid water, I paused at the sound of a child's laugh. Of course, children laughed in eternity, just not at the river's edge. The river banks were reserved strictly for drop-offs. Perking up, I whipped my skull around.

On the misty banks of the afterworld, a small boy ran laughing and screaming, dressed in gray plaid knickerbockers and a chocolate brown newsboy cap. An old man, also with mirth in his eyes, chased him.

Upon a closer look, it became evident who the young boy and the old man were. My jawbone fell open. The souls were none other than Tiny Tim and Ebeneezer Scrooge. Rosy-cheeked and healthy as can be, Tiny Tim no longer relied on his makeshift crutch. Apparently, his rickets had been healed by a pleasant dip in the healing pools of eternity.

And Scrooge, that crotchety old man whose soul I'd picked up over a century ago, ran after the little boy in an equally jovial mood. Living in the idyllic afterworld, full of joy and comfort, had done wonders for his soul.

Watching the scene, I wiped away a tear from the corner of my eye socket.

As I placed my hand bone over my rib cage, a gruff voice yelled, "You can't run here after hours!"

I twisted my neck bones to see who would stoop to admonish the innocent Tiny Tim. I peered into the fog. Chasing after the young boy and old man was Moe, the spirit guide.

My eye sockets narrowed. Ah, yes, the spirit guide with the less-than-stellar customer service. Granted, he had a job to do and was doing it. But he could've handled it more tactfully. Excellent customer service took priority in the afterworld. We did our best to promote the well-being of souls who'd journeyed here. Eternity was in the business of soul-oriented service, after all.

Still laughing, Tiny Tim and Ebeneezer Scrooge disappeared into the fog. Moe, too, was no longer in sight. The banks of eternity quieted down.

I let out a wistful sigh, then grabbed my wooden oar and rowed my tottering boat over the calm, hazy river, returning to headquarters to finish the workday.

Laughter and merriment had spread through all corners of the office. The staff were engrossed in a game of Never Ho-Ho-Have I Ever. Most of the employees' fingers were down, leaving a few potential winners. One of them blurted out, "Never have I ever told Earthly children that Santa wasn't real."

I crept past, hoping they wouldn't drag me into their festive game.

"Reaper!" Larry shouted.

Snapping my finger bones, I halted mid-track and cautiously turned.

"Come on, be a part of the game," the spirit guide said with an animated grin.

"I've got things to do," I said. "You know, afterworld stuff."

"Just one question," he babbled over the group's boisterous giggles. "It'll be fun!"

"Reaper, reaper, reaper," the whole gang sang in unison.

I rolled my eye sockets and sighed. "Okay. Just one." I nudged my way into their circle and held up all ten finger bones.

"Never have I ever kissed someone under mistletoe," Cassandra said, her rosy cheeks growing even redder.

Everyone put one finger down, except me.

"You've never kissed someone under mistletoe?" Larry asked, all the while covering his mouth, pointing at me with one finger, and laughing.

"What's the big deal? No, I haven't. It's not like I'm James Dean. I've got the face bones for radio."

The staff roared. My ear bones turning red, I quickly got up and left.

I swung by the boss's office to wish him good night before heading out for the day. It was a courteous habit I'd acquired after working for him for seven hundred years. His door stood ajar, which was typical. What was not so normal was the strong whiff of bubblegum mixed with spicy notes emanating from inside. Like gin and tonic, I put two and two together. Death had been drinking spiked eggnog.

Poking my skull through the doorway, I caught the sight of empty bottles of eggnog lying on his desk and those that had rolled across the floor. Granted, sipping alcoholic eggnog was an appropriate and even delicious way to celebrate the joyous season, but drinking tons wasn't the wisest move.

I inched the door open and moved closer to his massive, motionless body. "Eh, he must be sleeping it off," I muttered to myself. "Can't have too much eggnog. Or can you?"

He probably just needed a few minutes to unwind with a few eggnog shots at the end of a long day. Scheduling final exits was never an easy task, and the holidays complicated matters.

Not knowing what to say—he couldn't hear me anyhow—I left and sauntered to my desk. I pulled out my phone to check my list of clients, a daily, end-of-day practice I'd developed to ensure I'd left no soul painfully lingering, uncertainly and painfully, in limbo. Scrolling through my device, I made a hard stop at one particular name, a very familiar name: one that turned me green with envy.

My brow bones knitted together, and I drew in a sharp breath.

I figured I was seeing things, forcing me to triple-check my latest schedule. Clear as vodka, Santa Claus's name stood out at the top of the list. I took a slight step back, nearly stumbling over my chair. My rib cage tightened. Did Death make a mistake? Errors were entirely possible, especially when the boss was drunk on intoxicating eggnog.

Death's fingers could've slipped as he drank and drank, growing tipsier. Mistakes in scheduling didn't happen too often in the grand scheme of things, but they did occur once in a while. No matter how infrequent, glaring errors like these made my skeleton buckle.

The jolly old man's name was on my list, scheduled to be picked up on December 24th.

As my abdominal cavity churned, I scrolled through the attachment to the notes section. Santa was to perish in a fierce blizzard at the North Pole on Christmas Eve. His elves, and the entire gift factory, would succumb to the massive storm, leaving nothing behind but an unforgettable whiteout of epic proportions.

I looked up. If I was scheduled to collect Santa's soul on Christmas Eve, that meant no one would get presents on Christmas Day.

No matter how I detested Santa and the holiday joy I never felt a part of, a tiny voice inside me screamed something was amiss.

Wasn't Santa supposed to live forever?

Over the centuries, he'd never grown older than his sixty years. He'd never gained one more wrinkle, or lost one more curly strand in his perfectly trimmed fuzzy white beard. The jolly man in red was stuck at a ripe, eternal age: the age he'd been given the gift of immortality.

I scratched my skull.

Mighty Death could do anything. He wielded immense power, sharing it with his eternal companion, Life. He held the authority to wipe out immortals, even Santa. After all, Death was a mere few rungs under the all-powerful Cosmic Light, whose presence made me want to hide behind my office chair.

The boss planned to wipe out Santa, not by old age or a bout of pneumonia or falling into a pond while ice skating on thin ice—but by being buried in a horrible blizzard. And all of Christmas would go with him!

I needed to sit down. I felt for my chair and leaned back in the creaky seat, trying to process the gravity of the situation. Death was canceling Christmas by scheduling Santa's final exit. No more ugly sweater stations, no more mind-numbing holiday music, no more enticing aromas of Life's gingerbread cookies. I felt torn between the good and the mildly exasperating. The boss must've made a terrible mistake.

I got up from my seat and marched to Death's door. I'd ask him straight out if he was sure about his decision. But when I reached, the boss still hadn't awoken, much less moved an inch.

Rubbing my chin bone, I began to imagine a world without Santa. I'd never again be disappointed about not getting anything good for Christmas. I'd never feel irked when he was greeted with cookies and milk while I was met with garish screams and feet scrambling in the opposite direction. Maybe in the absence of him and all the joy he represented, I'd veer away from my cantankerous grimness around the holidays.

Like the calm glow from a gentle sunrise, a change of heart overcame me. The idea of my nemesis passing grew increasingly appealing.

I shrugged. It was settled. I'd take the schedule at face value and pick up Santa's soul in two-and-a-half weeks.

The beginnings of a mischievous smile spread across my face bones. I rubbed my hand bones together, anticipating collecting my very special upcoming client. The object of my envy was about to be wiped out.

Nothing could make Christmas better.

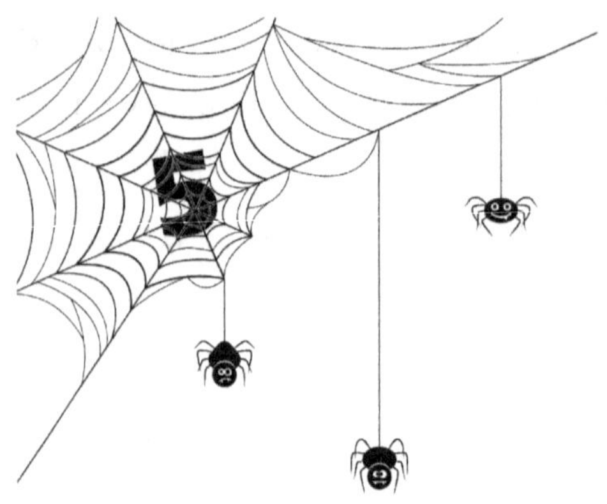

Picking up Santa's soul was a monumental job, considering the world treasured him. Everyone, young and old, was familiar with his affable nature, his twinkling gaze, his jolly laughter. Plus, they all expected him to deliver presents by shimmying down the red-brick chimney.

Not only was he a major, prominent figure, but the jolly old man entertained a huge labor force of elves. No one knew the official count, but it'd been estimated that he employed hundreds of thousands to tirelessly work the assembly lines in his massive gift factory.

The blizzard Death had planned for the North Pole was on the vast scale of his devastating tsunamis and earthquakes that had wiped out hundreds of thousands of living beings in the blink of an eye. Catastrophic disasters like these kept me busy collecting souls for a very long time. No doubt, once Death's Christmas Eve blizzard struck the North Pole, I'd be swamped with the hefty task of transporting thousands of souls—most elves—to the other side.

I took deep breaths, dwelling on how to successfully perform my duties. Perhaps I'd swoop down on Christmas Eve and collect Santa's soul as it hovered in shock over his suited body buried beneath fifty feet of snow, then do the same for his countless elves. I might have to inform Santa that my tiny boat couldn't accommodate his precious sled, so he'd have to leave it behind under the mountains of snow. He might argue or simply end with a cheery, "Ho, ho, ho."

Shaking my skull, I scrapped the idea. The herculean task of collecting Santa's soul required equally herculean preparations. I rolled up my cloak sleeves and raised my chin bone.

For this very special pickup, I'd digress from my typical way of collecting souls, which consisted of grab and drop, maybe with a bit of polite chitchat during the boat ride.

But Santa Claus was a colossal figure, cherished like the world's own lovable grandpa. He was respected, adored, praised, and anticipated every single winter without fail.

How could I give such a notable soul the same standard, *blah* treatment I gave other souls? No, an important client like him required a celebratory approach.

With my feet bones jittering, I considered my choices. I could simply appear at the North Pole as I did to pick up my ordinary clients. Or, at this time of year, I could fly on a helicopter to the pickup spot. I kicked my foot bone. It'd be too insignificant to do either. I'd quickly forget the blasé experience.

What made me bounce from foot bone to foot bone was a third option: dog sledding to the North Pole.

I began pacing back and forth, planning the ultimate pickup.

I'd assemble a pack of huskies to pull me and my sled to my destination, giving me oodles of fun along the way. In fact, I was ready for an adventure in a winter wonderland. I hadn't had one in eons. My work never took me to the North Pole, as Death had never before scheduled clients for pickup at the top of the world, where its only inhabitants were immortal.

I sighed with satisfaction. Yes, I'd take the fun, scenic route to collect my nemesis's soul.

It'd be harder, but worth the gargantuan effort. I'd remember the pickup forever.

At once, I began the extensive preparations. I rummaged through my closet and gathered a few cold-weather necessities: a face bone glove, chemical hand bone warmers, and plenty of extra layers. I bit down a smile when I found an old orange tent to set up camp, and sporks with which to nosh on my food. Speaking of food, the dogs would need animal proteins, so I picked up some meaty morsels from the pet store for my canine team.

The local mushers eyed me strangely, but I negotiated trained sled dogs on my way back. My adrenaline pumping, I secured seven sixty-five-pound Alaskan Huskies, who displayed patience, obedience, and intelligence—three qualities critical for an inexperienced reaper about to mush a highly energetic pack of dogs across a dangerous mess of snow and protruding ice. I picked up a few commands from the musher, like "Hike!" to get them moving and "Whoa!" to slow them down. I learned about the dogs' good and bad habits and felt confident to mush the dogs to the North Pole with as few hiccups as possible.

I'd need skis to guide the dogs. I brought out my ski equipment from the dark recesses of the storage compartment. My empty insides vibrated as I blew off the thick layer of dust off and wiped away the tangled cobwebs clinging to the skis—which completed my gear.

Next, I plotted my destination: 90 degrees north latitude.

The sun began to set, leaving an orange haze outside my frosty window. I yawned big and stretched my arm bones wide. Preparing for a major client pickup took more out of me than I expected. It wasn't every day that legendary souls arrived at the top of my list.

My bed looked cozier than ever. I dropped onto the soft, oversized mattress, let my feet bones dangle over the edge, and covered my tired skeleton with the sheets. I sank into the bed, snug as a cocoon.

First thing tomorrow morning, I'd set out with the dogs on my seven-day solo expedition to the magnificent and exclusive North Pole.

"Hike!" I yelled to the huskies I'd harnessed before dawn. The team of dogs began to pull the sled. As it slid across the snowy path, I jumped onto the back.

Eh, dog sledding was a piece of cake.

We mushed through forests of lush trees with their needles drooping with snowfall, over gently rolling hills, and down cascading valleys. My senses heightened as we sped through the picturesque winter wonderland. I'd never known the icy sights of winter could appear so pleasing. Maybe because I'd never cared to spend too much leisure time in minus ten-degree weather.

I closed my eye sockets, feeling the wintry breeze blowing across my skull bones. The air smelled clean as a brand-new day. A relaxed smile crossed my face bones.

Over the next twelve hours, the dogs pulled my 200-pound skeleton 45 miles without tiring. I wanted to give them a round of applause, but opted for the more practical move of keeping my grip on the reins.

We stopped every three hours so they could refuel with scraps of food and a much-needed rest. Three hours later, we resumed our journey. Three hours of travel followed by three hours of rest took us far.

The purplish evening descended like a misty fog, creating low visibility levels. “Haw!” I yelled, commanding the huskies to turn to the left to avoid a steep cliff I'd nevertheless spotted up ahead. The last thing I wanted was to plunge skull-first down a hundred-foot ravine to my second death.

Obedient and still vigorous, the dogs swerved in the nick of time.

Night fell soon thereafter, prompting me to shout, “Whoa!” The dogs stopped in an expansive clearing where I set up camp, lit a fire, and fed my weary bag of bones with broth and cuts of meat. The huskies had their fill of meaty tidbits in a hydrating soup, along with enough sleep to rejuvenate them.

Early the next day, we set out again amid freshly fallen snow and on an unbeaten path.

And so it went for four full days and nights.

A little over halfway through the expedition, we approached a pressure ridge. It became necessary to guide the huskies over the unpassable areas filled with large amounts of broken ice. I hopped off the sled and began chopping away at the rough ice with an ice pick.

I panted heavily, with condensation from my breath freezing in midair. The new physical demands on my skeleton led to an uneasy soreness. My skeleton never got used to the strain as I cut away at the ice.

The grueling work took hours before it was manageable enough for the dogs to cross. Humph. I'd thought the dogs did all the work, that I'd just have to stand on the sled and yell commands.

But I was as wrong as a wrong way sign on a highway, and my achy back made that clear.

Wiping my brow bone, I sighed and stomped back on the sled. The dogs continued pulling.

Hours later, the path demanded we maneuver over newly frozen open water. The dogs sensed the cracks in the ice before I had a chance to see them. I probed the ice with my ski pole, discovering the surrounding ice was too thin to cross. The canines had stopped before falling in.

I glanced skyward with my hand bones clasped, then reached out and patted the dogs' furry heads.

Despite rowing a boat across a river every day as a part of my professional duties, I'd never been much of a swimmer. I hated to think about the consequences if I ever fell in. But the dogs saved us, the mission, and my gear. I breathed a sigh, relieved to have picked smart huskies to traverse the hidden dangers on the way to the North Pole instead of an ignorant snow machine.

By now, I'd grown weary. Languishing at the reins, I needed to be in better shape than I was. Driving a dog sled demanded high level of physical exertion and mental fortitude–none of which I had based on my sheer exhaustion four days into the journey. I barely had the skill to regulate my skeletal temperature, which made me feel colder than was comfortable in these extreme conditions.

Three more days of driving the sled seemed insurmountable. I couldn't do it. I was too exhausted. Even setting up camp at nightfall took tremendous energy after mushing all day. With me catching a mere three hours of Zs in bitter temperatures, sleep deprivation took its toll.

"Easy!" I cried out, slowing the pack down. We traveled through a seemingly endless forest, pine trees crowding us on either side. The dogs had the ability to navigate through the thick woods, but I lacked the motivation to continue.

The huskies pulled the sled, but at a slower pace. The day grew dimmer, grayer, and increasingly morose.

A sense of emptiness grew in my abdominal cavity. My focus was off, dangerous in conditions where it needed to be sharp. Apathy overcame my weary skeleton.

Why was I doing this? Just to pick up a jolly old soul whose time had finally come?

Humph.

I could've easily swooped down on Christmas Eve and been done with the task. But no, I decided to take the adventurous route to collect my nemesis's soul. My nasal cavity flared. A rival who worked one day a year, while I slaved away every minute. A rosy-cheeked arch enemy who displayed charming gaiety at all hours, while I remained as grim as a thundercloud.

Glaring into the putrid blackness of the night, I bared my set of pearly whites. My eye sockets grew flinty.

Santa was offered warm mince pies and sherry, while I got nothing, nada, zilch. Not even a frosted shortbread skeleton cookie and a warm soda. Humph. All the health-conscious folks would leave him celery sticks and tomato juice—served him right.

I ground my teeth, knowing Santa was supported by hundreds of thousands of spirited elves, while I worked solo without the help of even a part-time administrative assistant.

To top it all off, the man in red never felt the unbearable pangs of loneliness. He was wrapped up in the wholesome adoration of the lovely Mrs. Claus, perpetually smitten by him. Good ol' me didn't even get a homely Mrs. Reaper to dote on.

My fury surged. "Hike! Hike! Hike!" I yelled as loud as I could, my booming echoes shaking the snow off the tree branches.

We tore through the forest and beyond, traveling at the fastest speeds of our entire journey.

"Gosh, is it dark," I said as soon as I reached 90 degrees latitude—the North Pole. I jumped off the sled and unharnessed the dogs, letting them roam.

In every direction I turned, a blanket of darkness engulfed me. I glanced at my smartwatch. Four o'clock in the afternoon, and the blazing sun was nowhere in sight. Apparently, the ball of fire dipped below the horizon and stayed there 24/7 during the polar night.

My skeleton shivered in the minus forty-degree chill. The nippy air burned a little in my throat bones. Good thing I was mere bones—anything else in these harsh conditions would've turned black and fallen off. Teeth chattering, I hugged myself. But the iciness penetrated deep into my core.

First thing on my mind: shelter from the biting cold. I stomped through twelve inches of snow over the six-foot-thick ice floe, eyeing my surroundings for the smallest sign of civilization. Despite my yearning to be near a society bustling with activity, I could see nothing but snow drifts. No wonder Death never sent me here. With no one around, not a soul needed collecting.

About two hundred years ahead in the ice desert, my eye sockets caught the sight of a yellowish flicker. It drew me closer, like a fluttering moth to a flame. I trudged through the knee bone-deep snow, huffing and puffing, as fast as the snow drifts would let me, all while thinking how traditional Alaskan snow shoes would've done me good right now.

As I approached the light source, I couldn't contain a small grin. I'd finally made it to some sort of arctic civilization that had survived, despite being established in a subfreezing no man's land. Squinting, I made out a tiny structure. It was white and circular, and blended in with the surrounding blankets of snow.

Mere steps away, it became clear the yellow flicker was a flame at the tip of a thin, beige wax candlestick, which stood in the middle of a windowsill of an igloo. Outside the igloo was a red-and-green sign with the words *North Pole Inn.*

I did a double take. An inn at the uninhabitable top of the world? How often did the North Pole get tourists?

I stared blankly at the snow-whipped building.

Finding no answers, I swung open the snow block door and walked inside. The place, toasty as an oven, was alive with music and merriment and the glow of yellow lights.

The ice crystals that had formed on my brow bone melted instantly. A warmth spread through my rib cage. What a welcome contrast to the bleakness outside.

I wiped the snow off my feet bones on the red Nordic forest mat at the front entrance.

"What can I do fer ya?" asked a pipsqueaky voice.

I jerked my skull around to see no one in front of me. I began taking quick breaths, feeling sweat accumulate on my hand bones. Was the North Pole some magical, haunted wonderland?

Then I felt a gentle tug at the bottom of my cloak. I looked down to see a little elf dressed in green with red-and-white striped stockings covering his spindly legs. Pressing my hand bones against my rib cage, I let out a slow exhale.

"Need a room?" he asked with a smile almost bigger than his wee, childlike face.

"Oh, he-he." I scratched my skull. "Um, yeah, I guess. I won't be staying long. A week, no more than that. Job's sent me here, and once it's done, I'll be leaving."

"Coming right up!" he squeaked. He plucked a set of keys from a wooden board hanging on the wall of snow behind him and handed them to me. "Second igloo on the right. Enjoy your stay!"

I accepted the keys. What a nice guy. It's too bad the elf was probably among my list of upcoming clients.

Keys in hand bone and chin bone up, I sauntered back into the dark freeze. Up ahead and to the right stood my one-reaper igloo, just as the cheery elf had said.

I pushed open the snow block, greeted with a twin-size bed, a small rusty stovetop with one burner, and a tin coffee pot next to it, as well as a freshly cut block of ice that must've been some sort of frigid seating area. I dropped my scythe with a clank and collapsed onto the bed.

The next morning appeared no less dark than the night before. Yet I awoke. I'd enjoyed a long, restful, and much-needed slumber. I stretched my arm bones and smacked my dry jawbone.

A bit of fresh Arctic air would do me good. With a crisp nod, I strolled out the snow door to the backyard. Over to the side of the snowy patio sat a small box. Brow bones raised, I moved closer to examine the contraption.

Inside, a package of hot dogs, a big bar of chocolate, a box of honey graham crackers, and a bag of jumbo marshmallows sat neatly arranged on two glass shelves. It was a mini fridge, with no need for ice or electricity. Perishable food stayed perfectly chilled in the perpetual frigidness.

"Just what I need." I clapped my hand bones and went to prepare my first snack at the North Pole. I only wished the fridge had come stocked with beer too. I salivated for a few bottles after my arduous trek.

Lighting a crackling fire with the pile of logs in the center of the snow patio, I seated myself on a green patio chair. I attached the hot dogs to one of several long, wooden skewers I'd found next to the fridge and cooked them over the open flame.

After gobbling up the warm hot dogs, I roasted the marshmallows, then sandwiched them between the chocolate and two graham crackers. I mustered a grin, despite the marshmallows and chocolate getting stuck on the roof of my mouth. As I enjoyed my morning campfire dessert, I leaned back and gazed upward.

A spectacular sight unraveled before my eye sockets. Brilliant green and purple hazes danced across the darkened sky. The northern lights looked more stunning than ever from my unique vantage point. I tipped my neck bone back to take in their full glory. I couldn't help but remain still as a corpse, unwilling to let anything, even a tiny skeletal movement, interrupt my surreal moment.

I sat entranced for hours under the shimmery lights undulating across the sky like majestic wave crests in a volatile ocean. I'd never realized such beauty existed at the North Pole. No wonder Santa made his home here. I'd always thought he'd been exiled to the top of the world for no good reason.

Although it seemed like pure constant night, the atmospheric beauty was far greater than mere speculation. The range of lights and colors in the exuberant sky bounced off a variety of sources and changed continuously, creating breathtaking views I dared not miss.

Granted, the North Pole didn't boast of significant solar light in mid-December, but the lunar light and hundreds of millions of stars grew even more luminous against the backdrop of the night sky.

After gobbling up my delicious snack, I sat relaxed, absorbed in the strangeness of my environment. Unlike being in other parts of the world, here I couldn't smell a thing, not stinky walruses, not polar bears emerging from their dens, not even hardy vegetation. Anything that could emit a scent was frozen, as if in a timeless state.

I found myself on repeat, saying, "Wow."

The sheer quiet struck me too. Birds didn't chirp. Arctic animals didn't scurry across the snow. All the wildlife had escaped for the winter, making the landscape deafeningly silent.

So quiet that I felt utterly present in the moment.

Then goosebumps slid along the back of my neck bones. With my senses heightened, my ear bones did pick up a faint clamoring sound in the far distance. I turned my skull to see what I could hear. But a purplish blackness, lightened only a smidgeon by the cascading aurora borealis, met my eye sockets.

I got up from the chair and wandered a few hundred yards out into the vast snowy wilderness.

That's when it became clear what the noises were—the clink-clank of Santa's gift factory, down yonder.

I returned to my igloo, now frozen over with a layer of ice. The ice cover acted as a sort of insulator, keeping the insides of my room cozy to a degree reasonable for the Arctic.

In the corner lying against the snow wall, I found a pair of traditional wooden snowshoes. Woven like fish net over and through wooden frames, they came in a nesting shape. The pointed tail allowed for efficient walking through a foot of snow. I planned to take a serious trek across the Arctic, and needed the gear to make it happen. The innkeepers had anticipated the same, and accommodated their guests.

My adrenaline pumping, I strapped the snowshoes onto my feet bones and trudged outside. At this high latitude, the wind blew predominantly Eastward. Fortunately, the wind was light. But strong gales from the previous night had formed large snow drifts over which I had to traverse.

I began the trek. Walking in these snowshoes was awkward. I wobbled with each step as I sank twelve inches into the fluffy snow. Hiking poles would've been advantageous, but I hadn't noticed any in my room. I clenched my jawbone and cursed under my breath.

Breaking a trail took immense effort, even with the snowshoes' broad surface area. With every lift of my feet bones, the snow fell through the openings in the woven snowshoes.

More than once, I threw my arm bones into the air, on the brink of giving up.

Despite scrunching my face bones and trying hopelessly to maintain my balance, I was determined to peek inside Santa's gift factory. It'd be wiped out by Death's upcoming blizzard, so I wanted to have a look before it crumbled into eternal oblivion.

I stomped a mile through the deep snow, teeth bared before the rattling and tinkling noises grew steadily louder. The tension released from my skeleton. Within the hour, I made out a faint yellow light in the distance. I slapped my hand bone over my jawbone.

A tall, three-story silvery building came into view. Half-moon, floor-to-ceiling windows decked each of the three floors.

I took a deep breath. The structure was full of old-world charm, as if straight out of a classic fairytale.

At the very top of the gift factory, a large sign appeared with white backlit letters that read *Santa's Workshop*. I was certain it could've been seen for miles, if it weren't for the ongoing gusts of blinding snow.

Beneath it, a smaller mahogany sign read *Hot Chocolate Factory*. The delicious chocolate scents wafted into my nasal cavity. It was the first thing I'd smelled all day. The aroma was pure delight: grandma's country kitchen. I'd couldn't remember a Grandma Reaper being a part of my existence, but I figured such a matronly figure might've prepared warm mugs of boozy hot chocolate instead.

My attention turned to an elaborate round clock face gracing the top of the building. The long hand laid over the nine, and the smaller one over the six. Despite it being morning, I couldn't tell in the hazy darkness.

Attached to the first building was a second, also featuring several arch top windows. I felt like I was in the middle of a wintry dreamland. Nowhere in the bottom realms of Earth could I find quaint buildings of this caliber. The magnetic charm of it all drew me steps closer.

Colorful string lights and large wreaths hung outside the facades. Billowy gray smoke poured out of the half-dozen smokestacks jutting out from the rooftops. I wasn't too concerned about the pollution, since Europe sent over mass amounts from their continent to the Arctic.

I almost squealed at the uber-adorable elves standing on the balconies or poking their heads out of the windows and yelling at the workers on the sidewalk.

My breath froze in midair as I rubbed my cold finger bones. I'd done it: arrived at Santa's famed workshop. I squatted in the snow, taking in the sights of the endearing spectacle.

All I wanted was a good look inside. It wasn't every day that someone besides elves got to see the celebrated gift-making process, one that captivated the entire world at this time of the year.

With the elves busy chatting or hurrying inside and out, it became a challenge to achieve my goal unnoticed. A nine-foot-tall reaper cloaked in black, and moseying outside Santa's gift factory, didn't sit well with most folks. I got it. Even at my best, I had the reputation of being the harbinger of doom.

The bells, the honking of Fiats, and the rustling of wrapping paper enlivened the atmosphere with the festive spirit of the season. The high-pitched sounds produced in Santa's workshop were all my ear bones could hear in the otherwise deathly silent North Pole.

I crouched behind a snow-covered wooden barrel. An elf ambled past, whistling a tune and forcing me to duck lower. I bolted to a quieter and less-busy side of the workshop. Another elf walked out with a broom. He began sweeping the snow away from the doorstep. I plastered my cloaked skeleton flat against the building, holding my breath. He finished his chore and returned inside. With my hand bones on my rib cage, I let out an exhale.

The coast was clear, allowing me to slip under one of the arched windows. I raised my skull up, where from inside only my eye sockets could be seen at the bottom of the window sill from inside.

A golden light, warm as honey, bathed the interior parts of the factory. Off in the corner, a crew of elves experimented with test tubes, creating mini explosions bursting with gas and puffs of white smoke.

Glass bottles of olive oil moved down two assembly lines, as elves slapped labels on them that read *cold-pressed.*

"This is unbelievable," I whispered to myself, watching.

On a table, a group of elves assembled mini stoves, which served as makeshift firepits on dreary winter nights. Although I could light a fire outside my igloo, this little fire pit could produce a smokeless fire. My eye sockets sparkled. It was my second gift wish after the cocktail smoker kit.

I pressed my skull against the window.

Across from the group, another team stuffed 24 mini bottles of wine from France, California, and Italy into the round holes of a wine calendar. Whoever received this lovely gift would have the chance to sample wines of all varieties, from smooth reds to crisp whites. I gazed at it, smacking my jawbone.

One table over, elves hand-blew stemless wine glasses, likely to pair with the wine calendars. The handblown glasses were idyllic Christmas gift for vino-lovers, me included. Although, I preferred a gut-punching 192-proof vodka any day.

From air fryers to oversized cardigans and reading valets, the elves kept busy adding the finishing touches to these highly desirable holiday gifts. I turned away, almost wiping away a tear that had not yet fallen. Once the blizzard hit, no one would be getting Christmas presents. My shoulder bones slumped.

Then a bearded elf, looking very much like a miniature Santa, love handles and all, waddled past. I stood motionless and halted my breathing. He failed to notice me.

At once, it hit me like a knock-out jab to the face bones. Santa was the *real* reason I was here. I didn't need to feel bad about no one getting presents when not a soul bothered to give me even custom-made socks with my skull printed on them. I hadn't seen the likes of a cocktail smoker kit in recent times either.

I huffed and puffed and almost wheezed as I leaned my arm bone against the building. Fearing I'd make a scene and be discovered, I hurried away, beyond the snowbanks and back to my igloo.

While seeing the action inside the gift factory expanded my horizons, it unduly reminded me of my agonizing holiday joylessness and enduring loneliness. Staring dully into the void of the polar night, I sniffed and wiped my dripping nasal cavity with my finger bone.

Only one thing would make up for my disappointments this time of year—picking up my nemesis's soul.

A feeling of satisfaction overcame my skeleton, like a mug of hot cocoa on a blustery day or waking up on Christmas morning to a heaping pile of wrapped gifts, one of which included a cocktail smoker kit with a torch.

I made up my mind. Before his fateful day arrived, I'd make a trip to 123 Santa Claus Lane and see for myself what my arch enemy—the figure responsible for my holiday blues—was up to.

Dark and early the next morning, I dug out the remaining hot dogs from the crumpled package and heated and gobbled them up. My brow bones knitted. I hadn't seen a grocery store for miles around the North Pole, making me wonder where I'd get my next meal.

Eh, I'd worry about the vital need for food later. I had a bigger job: snoop around Santa's digs to satisfy my curiosity about the legendary figure who had everything—before Death obliterated him.

After strapping on my awkward snowshoes, I dug into my cloak pocket and pulled out my phone. GPS would give me clear directions to 123 Santa Claus Lane. The entire surrounding landscape was a blanket of snow, making it hard to get my bearings, much less be guided by a good sense of direction.

Santa's actual residence didn't appear to be in the vicinity—maybe his house was so grand it required its own magnificent street. My empty insides vibrated. His digs must've been bigger than a barndominium or a European castle without windows. I grabbed the side of my skull and slid my finger bones down my cheekbones.

There was only one way to find out the extent of Santa's luxury: travel to his den.

I entered his address into my GPS. It showed me multiple route options, all of which included crossing snowbanks, snow drifts, and miles of snowy gales.

Grunting, I confirmed the third route option. I lifted my eye sockets, gazed at the blinding squall before me, and began my trek.

The Arctic wind blew against my cheekbones, turning them into ice packs. I fought the bitter cold, emboldened by the fact that I'd soon fulfill the fantasy of every believer who fretted where they came down on the Naughty or Nice lists.

It was an unfair dynamic. No one wanted to be spied on all year long, at home, at work, at play. Me? Eh, I'd only be doing a little investigating of Santa's place as part of my job. Who knew where he'd be on the day of the blizzard? Perhaps under his sheets, which I bet were pure silk, or supervising his workshop.

As I trudged through the snow and against the beating wind, my expression grew grimmer. My soul turned as cold as the conditions around me.

Comparisons hurled through my mind, despite knowing that envy was the thief of joy.

With a sour expression, I contemplated Santa's travel opportunities. He crisscrossed the north, the south, the east, and the west delivering presents on a single night each year. Bah. I, too, considered myself to be a savvy traveler, picking up souls from every corner of the globe. But Santa's escapades were different—they inspired joy, while mine inspired dread.

My eye sockets tightened as the cold turned my breath shallower.

The jolly old man probably *ho-ho-ho'd* so much because he jet-setted to exotic locations, from wealthy landlocked countries to tropical islands. I'd heard traveling did wonders for reducing stress and anxiety, though I was yet to experience these benefits. Rather, the countless souls who turned ashen white at the sight of me tended to increase my stress levels. And folks wonder why I looked perpetually grim.

My movements through the snow grew stiff, as I attempted to control my fury.

By traveling in the fresh night air, Santa reduced his risk of a heart attack. My job, however, often took me to factories spewing thick, black smoke, where the rampant pollution increased my risk of the likes of a widowmaker heart attack—though I wasn't married, unlike Claus, and didn't have a beating heart.

I spat in the snow.

He learned about different cultures, traditions, and customs wherever his nighttime sojourn took him. Exposed to the rich diversity on the planet, Santa stepped out of his comfort zone, undergoing personal growth. Surely, he'd learned about himself in the process, and felt comfy with the legend he was.

Such thoughts left me unable to relax, and I pushed onward through the deep snow.

Granted, being swamped, he didn't do much communicating on Christmas Eve. But he did deepen his friendships with his team of reindeer. Having a friendly red-nosed reindeer for a pet offered irreplaceable benefits, including unconditional love and affection. Pet owners like Santa felt rushes of feel-good chemicals and grew resistant to germs. No wonder the common cold never kept him home on his showstopping night.

Bah, all I ever traveled with was my iron-cold scythe.

An ache started to form in my jawbone. I ignored it, letting my rage take its course.

Traveling all these centuries, entering a diverse array of homes, and sampling the treats left out for him must've given him precious memories he'd hold onto forever—or at least until the day of the blizzard.

I snickered. Santa displayed confidence, happiness, and creativity, while I, in comparison, was nothing more than a dark specter of grimness forced to abide by Death's strict rules.

The jolly old man in red was to blame for my unhappiness this time of year.

As I trekked farther, my feet bones sank six inches deeper into the snow. The drifts had gotten higher in these parts, making the journey more arduous.

I inhaled the cold, dry air, irritating my airways. With envy driving me, I pressed onward through the whiteout conditions, unable to see clearly but able to feel every icy snowflake landing on my bones.

I grumbled how privileged Santa was with flexible scheduling. He set his own hours outside of the twelve-hour window on Christmas Eve. He must've enjoyed amazing work-life balance and satisfaction. Unsurprising he'd remained dedicated to his job for centuries. His desirable work schedule decreased turnover and absenteeism. I'd never recalled a year when Santa failed to show up on Christmas Eve.

On the contrary, being a lowly staff reaper, I was forced to follow a daily, rigid schedule with little room for deviation. It wasn't like Death could schedule a passing on December second, and I had the leisure to pick up the soul on a more convenient day, like February tenth, leaving the confused soul in limbo for an uncomfortably long time.

The pain I'd nursed upon seeing Santa take pleasure in everything I wanted came out like polar bear claws. I shook my skull to try and rid myself of this growing resentment.

I glowered at his immense, enduring popularity. I, too, was famous the world over—but no one responded to me with mirth and gaiety. Understandably, he delivered joy, while I delivered fright. Still, Santa remained a renowned figure, admired by all generations. Folks, young and old, anticipated him every Christmas—sometimes even as far in advance as July.

My feelings of inferiority intensified. The wind howled. I checked my GPS. I was closing in on my destination.

The gusts felt bitter cold. I brought my hood over my skull. In doing so, my brooding took me to Santa's red velvet outfit—it never went out of style. The jolly old man was a fashion icon. For centuries, anyone with a head wore Santa's famous red-and-white cap during the holidays.

Of course, I got my special day on Halloween. But my tattered outfit stood in competition with hundreds of others, from Frankenstein to Dracula and ghouls who'd risen from the dead. If I were lucky, I'd notice a mere handful of trick-or-treaters dressed up as me—which wasn't exactly an honor to boast about.

But not Santa. He was the central figure every Christmas. No one competed with him. He was out of everyone's league.

I kicked the snow with the tip of my snowshoes and tripped over them, landing face bones first in the snow. Instead of hoisting myself up, I sat there sulking as the snow clung to my bones.

Humph. My envy would be over, I told myself, once the blizzard struck. My feelings of inadequacy would disappear.

Just then, a house came into view. My pulse raced.

I was nearing Santa's abode.

I lifted my skeleton out of my temporary snow grave. My pace quickened, but only slightly. Trekking through deep snow had reduced my normal speed.

Two large structures appeared. One took the shape of a mailbox, or more like a vault the size of a house. My skull flinched back. Inching closer, I realized the structure was indeed a mailbox, probably filled with hundreds of thousands of letters.

I smirked.

If only Santa upgraded from snail mail to email, he wouldn't worry about recycling all that paper. We made the upgrade at afterlife headquarters, and it'd saved us from chopping down a bunch of trees.

I stepped forward steadily, wondering if my letter was somewhere in that heap inside the mailbox.

I brushed off the thought. Cassandra was probably right. Santa letters were just a formality, and he'd never read them.

The second building looked more like a one-story home, decorated with red-and-white candy cane stripes and a dramatic, high thatched roof. A tall well-ornamented Christmas tree stood out in front. Two large candy canes guarded the front door. Green garlands with red bows lined the home's periphery. I'd heard that Christmas magic protected Santa's house. I'd soon see for myself if that were the case.

I crouched and made my way toward the home. Once I was within inches, I made myself small underneath the window, the frosty panes of which made it hard to see inside. Using the tattered edge of my cloak sleeve, I rubbed the frozen condensation in circles, dislodging it. The ice crystals fell away, giving me a clearer view.

Placing one hand bone over my brow bone, I peered inside. It was rather gloomy, dusty, and empty, not at all what I expected in the home of the jolliest man on Earth.

But I cocked my skull on seeing the silhouettes of a series of familiar objects: an old, round wooden dining table with a dozen empty beer bottles scattered across it.

I gasped and sprang back, falling sitbones first into the snow.

My abdominal cavity fluttered.

Santa—enjoyed a good beer?

With jerky movements, I shifted in the drifts, trying to get back on my feet bones. Amid my awkward struggle in the twelve-inch-deep snow, the metallic click of a lock sounded quick as a snap.

My ear bones perked up just before my eye sockets bulged. I laid my cold finger bones over my colder jawbone, my teeth chattering like a tap dancer's ball change.

Santa's wooden front door swung open slowly with a loud creak. I grew clumsier in the snow, trembling in my bones. At best, I expected a harsh scolding or, at worst, a dire warning about how he'd personally handle unwanted trespassers. Maybe he'd charge out with a semi-automatic rifle, cocked and ready to shoot and deliver me to my second death. My breaths became quicker as I looked for an exit route in the surrounding whiteout.

Or, maybe Santa's house really was protected by Christmas magic, and an infantry of armed diminutive elves strapped with crisscrossing belts of ammo, stood behind his door, prepared to launch a magical offensive attack on whoever compromised their dignity to snoop on their beloved Santa.

My teeth-chattering grew louder, more rapid. Still stuck in the snow, my skeleton froze, not because of the whipping cold but out of harrowing fear. It suddenly occurred to me how my clients felt when I arrived to pick up their soul.

The tip of his fuzzy white beard appeared first in the doorway. Moments later, the sight of a velvety red suit. Out stepped Santa, large as life and rosy cheeked as all the old-fashioned soda advertisements.

My mouth grew dry as a martini, and an empty feeling socked me in the pit of my empty gut.

"Ho-ho-ho, why you must be chilly down there in the snow," he said, belly bouncing and his eyes full of mirth.

"Wh-who me?" I asked in shaky voice.

"Yes, you. Why don't you come on in? Warm yourself up, and have a beer with me."

My teeth stopped chattering. Instead, my jawbone dropped to the snow-covered ground. I needed to sit down, but I already was. Santa wanted a drink—and with me?

He outstretched his fleshy hand, and despite flinching, I took it. With a robust strength I'd never expected in a man as ancient as he was, he hoisted me up and out of the snow. I let out a huge breath. After too many uncomfortable minutes sitting in the damp, freezing snow, it was refreshing to stand on my two feet bones again. I wiggled my skeleton, letting the snow fall off my cloak.

Santa led the way into his balmy abode, and I followed.

"Have a seat." He gestured toward one of the four wooden dining chairs I'd seen through the window. "You must be famished."

How did he know? Had he been snooping on me?

"Uh, yeah, actually, I am," I replied, pulling out the chair. "Haven't seen a grocery store or even a 7-Eleven for miles 'round here."

"That's the North Pole fer ya." He opened his white oven door and peeked inside.

I lifted my nasal cavity high in the air, smelling a delicious, smoky aroma. My empty insides growled with the promise of nearby food.

"Ham's just about ready," Santa said, putting on his thick green block print oven mitts. He pulled out a baked ham, and the salty and sweet aroma intensified a thousandfold.

He plopped the hot tray on the counter and reached for a silver carving knife and fork.

"How many slices?" he asked, throwing a kind glance in my direction.

I looked over to the countertop, salivating. The caramelized skin appeared baked to golden perfection, glazed with sweet brown sugar and honey. Just how I liked it.

"It's a honey and bourbon Christmas ham," he said, smiling. "Ten, twelve?" He must've read my hunger like his Naughty and Nice lists.

"Twelve slices, thin," I responded, smacking my jawbone.

He carved the ham and placed the slices on a plate, next to four thick yellow pineapple slices. He cut himself an equal amount, then walked over to serve me and himself at the table.

Santa plopped down on the seat across from me. Unabashed, I couldn't stop staring at him.

"Oh, how could I forget?" He hurried back to the kitchen and pulled out two bottles of chilled beer from the fridge.

Returning and handing me one, he held up his bottle. "Here's to the North Pole."

Still stupefied by his hospitality, I toasted with my beer.

He cut his ham into bite-size pieces and chomped. Feeling ravished, I followed suit. I hadn't eaten since morning.

"Mm. The ham's delicious," I said, through a sumptuous mouthful. "Did the little missus do the cooking?" I looked around, seeing no sign of Mrs. Claus. Not one velvet dress, not one curly wig, not even a red lipstick case.

Santa continued to stuff his mouth with forkfuls of warm, delicious ham. He shook his head, jiggling his lengthy white beard. "No, no," he said, chomping. "Mrs. Claus and I live separately."

I halted my fork midair and paused my chewing. My gaze went flat.

"We only come together for the show of the holiday season."

"You do?" I sat limply.

"Yep. There's only so many adventures we can share over centuries. After all this time together, we've simply grown tired of each other and choose to live apart." He looked at me from under his bouncing bushy white eyebrows. "Relationship burnout. It's a thing."

He left me speechless. Never in my wildest imagination did I think that Santa and Mrs. Claus would be on rocky terms. They'd looked so happy together in all the pictures. Smiling, cuddling, it was true love—or so it seemed on the surface.

Gregarious as he was, Santa popped another chunk of juicy ham into his mouth.

"You know, I let the missus trim my hair one time. Only once, mind you." He gave me a piercing look with his gray eyes. "She forgot to attach the blade guard to the trimmer. I ended up with a buzz cut. It took eleven months for my hair to grow back to its familiar glory. But it did, just in the nick of time for the holiday season." He shook his head. "I would've felt very bad going out with a buzz cut when everyone expected me with a head full of curly locks." He gave me a wink. "Thank goodness for Santa hats."

I remained still as a Christmas dill pickle ornament.

"There's only so many jokes I can tell after seventeen hundred or so years," he continued. "She's heard them all hundreds of times and no longer laughs. We've tried, but the fun just isn't there. All we've done for ages is bicker."

With a tinge of sadness, he looked down at his half-eaten plate. Sitting in silence, I offered him a thoughtful expression.

"We've run out of things to talk about," he said. "I've been at the same job year after year, supervise the same staff of elves, and ruminate on the same holiday problems I have to fix. Mrs. Claus–she still keeps her married name for the sake of appearances and contracts and stuff–has grown tired of hearing about all these mundane trivialities. She lives in Hawaii now for the year-round sunshine."

He let out a long, hapless sigh. Then he slowly cleaned the last tidbits of ham and chunks of pineapple off his plate. I did the same. He glanced over at his beer on the table and grabbed it. I raised a brow bone as he snapped off the crown bottlecap with his teeth. Taking my cue, I, too, opened my bottle with my set of pearly whites.

He guzzled his beer, patted his round belly, and let out a sigh of satisfaction. "Helps to know how to cook a good meal, eh? It's one of the finer aspects of existence. Makes the lonely nights worthwhile."

Lonely? Him too? My features softened, and I drank my beer heartily.

"You like video games?" he asked out of the blue as I helped him clear the table.

"Um, sure." I shrugged.

"Great, let's play." He sauntered to the living room as I followed while staring at the floor. My brow bones furrowed and released. I'd never known Santa was a passionate gamer. It wasn't in the literature.

He knelt over a shimmery gift-wrapped box in the corner, rummaged through it, and pulled out a game. "How 'bout 3D? If you can handle the lateral movements and the risk of motion sickness." He frowned, returned it to the box, and looked through more in his stash. "Or maybe *Existence is Strange*?" He held one up in front of his jolly face. "*Mario Cousins* sounds like a winner, eh?"

"Yeah, *Mario Cousins*. I like that. Let's play." I bounced my knee bones.

He set up the game. "You know, we wouldn't be playing if it weren't for Ralph."

"Who?" I asked, scratching my temple.

"Ralphie. These games were intended for him." He pointed to the wrapped gift box. "But he cheated on his wife."

"Noo," I said in a low voice, turning away and covering my jawbone.

"Yep, he cheated on her for months with his sexy young secretary. So I put him on my Naughty list. He's getting nothing for Christmas but a lump of coal." He handed me a set of controls.

Santa really did pay attention to who was Naughty or Nice.

We played *Mario Cousins* into the evening hours, talking about existence in between running out of lives, and forgetting to watch the time. The two of us shouted and whooped as if we'd known each other for eternity. Never did I expect it, but I was having the time of my existence.

With a sudden reverberating gong, the old grandfather clocked in Santa's hallway struck midnight.

"I better go," I told him.

"Ho-ho, you come back tomorrow, you hear?"

"First thing in the morning," I said, putting on my snowshoes.

I made the trek back to the inn, the whole time feeling a tingle in my rib cage.

The next morning, I flung off my bed covers with a wide, sparkly grin, feeling the most energized I'd been in a long spell of time. I'd been hanging out with Santa, and it warmed my empty insides like a hot toddy dribbling down my throat bones.

My abdominal cavity rumbled, reminding me that I had no food for the day. I swallowed excessively. How did the elfin innkeepers manage a stream of guests without a grocery store nearby or even a mobile food kiosk? The complimentary hot dogs and s'mores wouldn't satisfy guests for more than a half-day.

I shrugged off my concern. With my rib cage out and my chin up, I was sure as presents delivered on Christmas Eve that I'd find food at my destination: Santa's house.

Taking easy breaths, I strapped on my snowshoes and swung open the door, only to be greeted by tempestuous winds and a glacial temperature of minus forty degrees.

I wrapped my arm bones snug around myself, a chill running down my bone-cold, well, bones.

Heading for Santa's temperate abode, my grumbling tummy drove me across the high snowbanks and over the rugged hills of the vast tundra. I leaned forward, remaining attentive as every bumbling step sank my leg bones deeper into the snow. The last thing I wanted was to be stuck, starving, and struggling to move in the middle of this frigid, silent wasteland where not a cry could be heard for miles.

I pushed onward. The trek seemed to be shorter this time around, even though the distance and icy conditions remained the same. Perhaps time sped by as I grew distracted by my gnawing hunger. Or maybe I felt optimistic about meeting up again with the jolly old man.

Whatever it was, adrenaline pumped through me.

Four thousand awkward snowshoe steps later in the fluffy snow, Santa's red-and-white residence rose up in the distance like a warm-hearted savior, ready to whisk me out of the chilling cold. I gazed ahead alert and hastened my steps in the dark early morning hours.

Nearing his residence, I felt a sensation of floating over the snow, as if all my worries had disappeared. Maybe Christmas magic did exist.

The wind whipped across my face bones and returned me to my harsh wintry reality. I knocked thrice on his front door. I didn't wait long in the cold, as Santa opened it in a matter of seconds.

"Ho-ho-ho! You've returned, jolly good Reaper," he said with a cheery laugh and ushered me in. Red suspenders supported his red velvet pants, into which he'd tucked his big white long-sleeved tee.

No one had ever called me "jolly." I sniffled.

Escaping out of the cold, I hurried into the coziness of his home and took a welcome gasp of humid, heated air. It moistened the back of my sinuses, which helped me breathe easily.

A fire crackled in the red-brick fireplace as I undid my snowshoes. The light, steady popping sounds from the dancing flames relaxed me to the bone.

Santa opened the fridge. "Hope you don't mind eating a little light this early in the morning."

"Anything'll do," I replied, tipping my skull back and closing my eye sockets. "Even a morsel would taste splendid with your fine culinary touch."

Santa laughed in his customary grandfatherly way and thanked me.

He brought out a tray of deviled eggs sprinkled with bright-red paprika along with a steaming dish of green bean casserole and a plate of crispy spanakopita. My eye sockets widened at the sight.

Opening the oven, he placed the smorgasbord of holiday delicacies inside. He set the timer for ten minutes and turned his attention to me.

"Just a few tasty snacks to start our day," he said with a grin. His plump, rosy cheeks shone.

My insides warmed at the thought of sharing food with the jolliest man I'd known.

"You made this entire spread today?" I asked with wonder.

"Well, when you've got nothin' else to do, you have time to whip up a whole lot." He winked.

Before I could ask another pointed question, the timer buzzed. Santa donned his oven mitts and pulled out the feast. Before he set the last dish on the table, I began devouring the delicious tidbits like a hungry Christmas wolf.

I asked him for his recipe for deviled eggs. Creamy and flavorful, I'd never eaten anything as tasty.

"It's all in the mayo," he said. "Homemade does the magic."

I gobbled up my last sumptuous half egg and turned to the window. The wind howled like a beast, perilously swaying the ornaments on the front lawn tree. The skies grew awash with hazy greens, purples, and blues–the breathtaking colors of the northern lights. Menacing as the land and sky seemed, I felt utterly safe, at home in Santa's dining room.

He glanced out the window too. "Seems like the perfect day to spend some time outdoors." He looked at me with a smile. "What'd you say?"

My posture bolted upright, and my bones visibly tightened. I'd just come out from the blustery snow and was rather enjoying myself in the comfortably heated sanctuary of sorts.

"Oh, don't mind a little Arctic cold," he said, making a dismissive gesture with his hands. His gray eyes glistened. "I've got just the trick to ease the scariness. Wait here."

He rushed over to his pantry and pulled out several packages of jumbo marshmallows, big as mini pillows, oversized bars of chocolate, and a box of honey graham crackers.

Making s'mores must've been a thing at the North Pole. Santa did say the comfort food eased the fright.

He gave a nod toward the food in his arms. "How 'bout it?"

"Uh-uh." I looked at the floor.

"Come on. We'll toast them in the fire pit outside."

"You've got a fire pit?" I asked, perking up.

"Yep, a nice big one, great for roasting a bunch of things."

I nearly fell out of my chair. "I'm down!"

Santa gave a joyful yelp, and we headed out to the back. My eye sockets bulged. Santa really did have a nice-sized fire pit in his backyard, complete with a heap of flavor-enhancing logs ready to be burned.

I tilted my skull to the side, admiring the large cast-iron fire pit.

“Eh, we could do with a lounge area,” he said, one hand on his hip as he eyed the surrounding snowy landscape.

I moseyed over, and we began piling up the snow. After fifteen minutes of shoveling and packing down the snow, we built a cozy snow lounge, complete with an ice-cold seating area and a table for two.

Santa kindled the fire with coals, which burned long and hot. I searched for thin branches, picked up two, and shaved off the ends to form a point. I handed him one and kept the other.

“I’ve got more coals if these run out,” he said. “Matter of fact, I’ve got bags upon bags of coals for all the naughty folks, plus extra for the fire pit!” He laughed boisterously, as his belly jiggled up and down.

I shook my skull while smiling in disbelief at my good fortune.

We sat around the fire pit on the snow lounge and stuck marshmallows on the pointy ends of the sticks. Holding them over the open flame, we rotated the gooey treats slowly, toasting them evenly.

I couldn’t contain my smile. Here I was, roasting marshmallows with the legendary Santa Claus, staring into the fire as if its heat would wake me up from this fantastical dream. I leaned back on the chilly snow lounge. Santa did the same. With our neck and neck bones tipped back, we gazed up at the shimmery northern lights dancing across the sky.

"Wonder what else is out there," he said, wistfully.

"Probably a lot more than the eye socket can see," I replied.

"Oh, how could I forget again?" Santa blurted out, shimmying up from his lounge seat. He trudged through the snow and into the house.

I sat rubbing my forehead bone. Moments later, he returned, pulling a traditional wooden toboggan sled through the snow. The load must've been heavy, because he used both hands to tug it to our lounge area.

In the darkness, I made out a mountain of glass bottles. As he neared, it became clear what they were.

My jaw dropped.

"A good drink never harmed nobody!" Santa said with a laugh, and grabbed two bottles of beer and a brandy for himself. With a clap of my hand bones, I trudged over and helped myself to a couple of ice-cold beers.

"That sure is a lot of liquor," I said, glancing at the heap, which glistened under the starry sky.

"Well, you know, a bit of brandy dulls the pain of loneliness."

Rubbing my rib cage, I could relate. With a small smile, I acknowledged our shared burden.

An idea hit me. I rose to my feet bones and began assembling nearby ice blocks in a row, stacking them one on top of the others. I carefully placed the many beer and brandy bottles on the flat ice surfaces. Once I finished, I stood back and admired my work.

Santa complimented my ice bar. A joyful whoosh tickled my bones.

"Plus," he said, "there's not much else to do 'round here the rest of the 364 days of the year but drink. My elves do all the work once I approve the Naughty and Nice lists, leaving me bored out of my mind until Christmas Eve. Then suddenly, I'm in demand and overworked through my Christmas Day shift. On Christmas, I'm wanted to lead parades across the world. I'm old and not in the best shape. I need a rest."

He looked at me with his weary gray eyes. "It really is exhausting."

As an on-demand reaper, I knew how he felt. I reached out to touch his sleeve.

Then I looked over at his sled. He followed my gaze. With a newfound pep in his voice, he asked, "You up for a game of Battleship?"

"Am I?" I replied, throwing my hand bones into the air. "I'd love to play."

Santa stretched out an arm to one side of his sled and retrieved the newly released electronic game, wrapped in pretty foil wrapping paper with a glittery blue bow on top.

"Was anyone too naughty to get the game?" I asked, pointing to the case.

"Ho-ho-ho." Santa laughed, unwrapping it and setting it up on the snow table. "Indeed, Mark should've received this shiny brand-new game. But he evaded his taxes, so he made it on my Naughty list."

I raised a brow bone.

We played, filling the night air with high-spirited hoots and hollers and yells of "Hit!" and "Miss!" until one of us sank the other's ship. Like the day prior, I enjoyed every bit of our guy time.

And I couldn't wait to come back tomorrow.

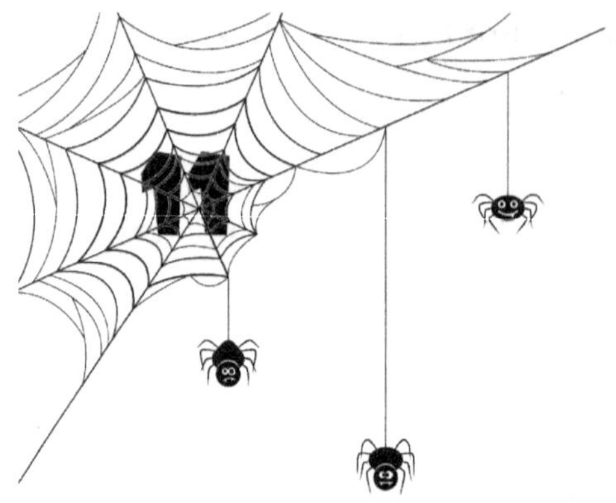

Waking in the dark dawn, I powered through the knee-bone-high snow and thick ice casing the Arctic badlands. Several steps away from Santa's place, a round red figure bobbed on his front lawn, next to an equally bright red yet motionless contraption. I squinted my eye sockets as I inched closer.

"Ho-ho-ho, Reaper!" Santa greeted me with a jolly grin once I neared. "Just polishing my sleigh. The busy season is in a few days. Must be prepared". In his gloved hands, he wielded a white rag covered with dirt stains. Indeed, driving a spotless, gleaming sleigh made it feel like driving a brand-new one.

The sleigh looked like a mean driving machine. It was a rustic metal contraption, designed to appear old-fashioned with its weathered finish. Maybe it was old, since Santa hadn't upgraded his sleigh in ages. Christmas would be ten times more charming with this flying through the moonlit skies.

"Man, what a ride." I fixed my gaze on the newly polished sleigh and walked around its four sides, their edges accented in gold, taking in its full glory. "It's all pimped out, too, with festive embellishments." I crouched, running my hand bones over the cold blades resting in the snow. "Ceramic composite?" I asked with a raised brow bone, referring to the blades.

"Yep, to withstand Arctic temperatures. The runners are smooth as can be to slide across ice and snow."

My eye sockets passed from the front tip of the shiny red sleigh to its end. "The sleek curves are rad."

"Well, rad they may certainly be, but they're essential to facilitate optimum airflow over them. They create just the right lift and keep the sleigh in the air." He stood back with his characteristic pleasant expression, watching me admire his red-hot ride.

Santa's shiny contraption featured double seating upholstered in black leather. The Arctic's moisture and cold must've done a number on the leather over the centuries, as foam poked out of two or three minor rips. I pressed one finger bone into the leather, and it bounced back. "Must be soft and comfy."

"Oh-oh," he said. "Soft as a feather and with an ergonomic design, perfect for my achy back." He placed his hand at the base of his spine and arching backward. "The seat height is adjustable, but I haven't needed to fiddle with it for centuries. If anything, after seventeen hundred years,

I'd only get shorter!"

"Still impressive."

"Let me show you the climate controls." Santa hurried toward the front and began explaining the controls while I stood next to the sleigh, admiring the technology. "This regulates the heat temperature, while that knob adjusts the fan speed."

"Probably don't need the fan, driving through the wind and all."

He laughed uproariously.

"You want to go for a ride?" His eyes twinkled like the stars above.

I dropped my jawbone and bounced from foot bone to foot bone.

"I thought you'd never ask!" I exclaimed, clasping my hand bones against my chest bones.

Santa made a clicking noise with his mouth, and his team of reindeer right away emerged out of nowhere and hopped into their correct positions before the sleigh. He harnessed the animals, then jumped inside. I followed suit and made myself comfortable in the seat next to him.

He yanked the reins hard. The sleigh became airborne, steadily climbing to ten-thousand feet. I peeked over the sleigh. I jammed my hand bones under my armpits as my breaths burst in and out. We crossed over flat expanses of land fringed with towering mountains. The trees, majestic on land, appeared as mere specks.

I kept glancing all around, especially behind myself.

The biting wind, feeling colder at this elevation, blew quietly over us. Santa responded to the wind gusts by driving the reindeers around them and accelerating their speed, which showed off his admirable expertise. Then we swerved beneath the swirling northern lights. Seeing them up close rendered me speechless. Not only did I see the aurora borealis, but I was actually in their midst, their light pulsating and snaking all around me. Its arcs and spikes, seemingly alive, grew intensely surreal at close range.

"It's out of this world," I said, holding on to my seat, with a pleasurable fright. Granted, though I traversed the cosmos to pick up souls near and far as part of my job, I'd never flown at this altitude in an authentic sleigh. Santa was no sissy, daring to soar ten-thousand feet in the thin air. Being pulled by reindeer upped the fun factor a million times over. Goosebumps formed on the back of my neck bones.

"You want to drive?" he asked out of the blue. Santa drove the sleigh in a fluid, relaxed manner. He made it seem effortless. I, however, had never even set my foot bones in a sleigh.

My eye sockets widened. "Me?"

Santa handed me the reins. "Sure, why not?"

"I-I guess I'll give it a try." Accepting the reins with hesitation, I shuddered.

I held on tight to the reins.

"Not too tight. Just enough to keep control," Santa advised patiently.

With the reins in my grasp, I made jerky movements. "Uh, do I need a seatbelt or anything?"

"Rudolph will keep us safe. Don't you worry about a thing." Santa's gentle words were intended to comfort. But reindeer added complexity to the drive. What if the reins got tangled? Or they started fighting midair? The massive, heavy antlers on these mysterious creatures were effective weaponry. A hundred concerns ran through my skull, despite Santa's words of encouragement.

But in no time, as we soared over the North Pole with the untamed wilderness opening beneath us, a feeling of weightlessness overcame my bones. A pleasurable freedom replaced my angst.

The sleigh moved at an astonishing speed. Rudolph took the lead, pulling with immense strength. Without warning, the sleigh accelerated–downward. A hollowness formed in the pit of my abdominal cavity. My hand bones grew sweaty, and I felt the reins would slip from my grasp at any second.

"Uh-oh, we're losing altitude," Santa cried out. "We need to climb. See that ridge over there?" He pointed to a snowy elevated landform on my right. I took sight of it.

"Yeah," I answered, my voice uncontrollably shaky.

"It's got a thermal lift. Let's fly over it." Santa directed me with calm and patience.

Trembling in my bones, I adjusted the reins, making a coordinated turn, and avoided the low spot. We gained altitude quickly. I breathed a long sigh and wiped my drenched forehead bone with the back of my hand bone.

The shock of nearly crashing into the mountains passed, followed by several glorious hours of uneventful flying. I learned how to control the sleigh, being able to maneuver the sleigh in any direction and, most importantly, predict its movements.

I sat with my shoulders back and my rib cage thrust out. A knowing grin spread across my face bones.

"Hey, this flying thing's no big deal," I said, looking over to see Santa's reaction.

"Once you get the hang of it, a sleigh ride through the sky is an unparalleled sort of magnificence."

I gave him a crisp nod, and held my chin bone high. As we flew, I felt at a sense of oneness with the sleigh as it flew through the sky alongside ivory gulls, the only birds that stayed in the Arctic despite the polar night. I reveled in overwhelming joy, unstoppable power, and the ultimate taste of freedom. I wished to stay in the air forever.

We glided across the dark, colorful open sky, the white blanket of snow sprawling below. The ride was silent, with nothing but the steady sounds of the howling winds, the tiny reindeer bells jingling, and the muffled hums and sputters of the hypnotic northern lights.

Whizzing through the air, I left the cosmos behind me, the frenzied transports of souls, and all my unending personal and professional worries. My stress vanished at this amazing altitude, and in the company of my unexpected new friend sitting shotgun beside me. It was a bliss I'd never exchange for anything else in the afterworld, and a peacefulness settled in my bones.

After hours of soaring pleasantly through the night skies, we landed behind Santa's home.

"I'd seen breathtaking views and felt extraordinary things," I exclaimed, leaping out of the sleigh with both feet bones at once. "It'll take me ages to process them all. The ride was a blast."

Santa gingerly exited from the side door. "Yeah, driving this sleigh is one of the highlights of my job. I just hope the thing lasts."

"What d'you mean?"

"Well, my sleigh is ancient and, like me, isn't in the best shape. It could go bust any holiday now. And then what'll I do?"

I stood silent, scratching my skull as a puff of my breath froze in midair.

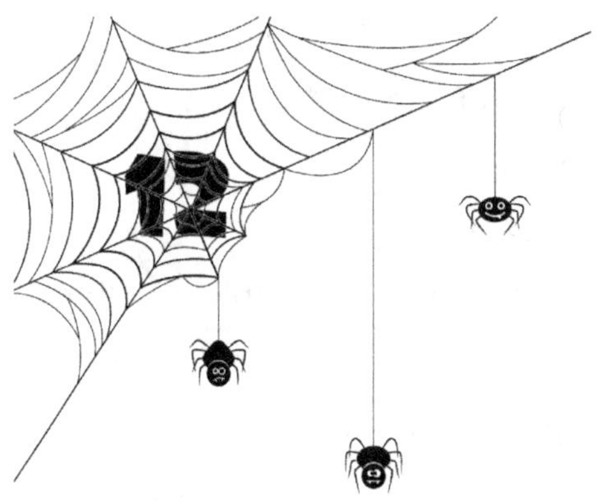

Warmth filled my bones, heading to Santa's place the next day. My empty insides felt so warm that the blustery Arctic chill failed to cause me the slightest discomfort. I kept a steady pace, when I heard the faint sounds of merry bells ringing from his workshop and felt a mild sense of grief, being separated from the jolly old man whom I now held so dear. I counted the minutes until I reached his abode.

As I traversed the snow drifts, I engaged in a bit of mental exploration.

A mere four days ago, I'd been tormented by burning envy. I'd long felt inferior to Santa, believing he had everything spectacular that I desired in all of existence. The envy inflicted on me an enduring pain—which felt almost like a physical pain—only because I decided that I was lacking.

The hideous envy squashed my self-esteem, inspired in me more grimness than I comfortably felt, and delivered an agonizing sense of emptiness.

How wrong I was to judge!

Santa had it as bad as me: the unbearable loneliness, the ancient, worn-out professional gear that could use an upgrade, and a penchant for strong drink when times got tough. Who knew Santa and the lovely little Mrs. Claus weren't on speaking terms, and only came together for show during the holiday go-time? With their smiling faces and rosy cheeks, the couple had always come off as convincingly happy together.

I rubbed my chin bone, still searching for answers. That Santa and Mrs. Claus lived separately shattered the idyllic picture that had tortured my mind. The outwardly smitten pair seemed destined to be together forever. But according to the man in red himself, the reality was far from fantasy.

I'd trudged a long distance from the inn, and could no longer hear the merry sounds from Santa's workshop. In fact, all my ear bones picked up were the whistling wind, my panting breaths, and the silence of the snowfall.

I returned to my contemplation. Santa and I experienced shared hardships and struggles. After the days we spent together hanging out chilling and talking, I felt shoulder-to-shoulder with the jolly old fellow. A camaraderie had developed between us. The two of us had become brothers. How many phantasmagorical specters could say they were good buds with Santa Claus?

A smile spread across my cold face bones. Feeling our bond of friendship, my genuine smile felt like it could last for eternity.

Over the past three days, filled with fun and clowning around, an unspoken commitment to one another had blossomed like a scarlet-red poinsettia. He looked out for me, and I did the same for him. That's what friendship was all about. It helped, too, that we enjoyed loads of spirited times together as pals.

I took deep, cleansing breaths. The air was chilly yet pure in these untouched parts of the North Pole.

My knee bones lifted high as I crawled over steep mounds of snow. My snowshoes sank deeper into the snow with each following step. I staggered forward, hoping to erase the distance between us.

Eh, I could've spent the entire day with him staring at a blank wall—and I'd still have had a good time. I felt centered in the moment, respecting the snowy icescape around me, despite it being a punishing obstacle course to navigate.

Maybe I'd have a heart-to-heart with Santa when we met up. Without compromising my masculinity or reaper dignity, I'd express my appreciation for our unlikely friendship, how our growing bond warmed me despite this being the coldest place on Earth. He did in fact save me from starving to a second death the first day. And his exquisite culinary skills hit the spot!

I smacked my jawbone just thinking about a golden baked ham, fresh from the oven, still sizzling.

Instead of him generously showering me with hospitality in the barren Arctic, I wished I could've bought a six-pack, showed up at his door, and spent the day getting drunk together. I looked up at the dark sky. But with nary even a convenience store in sight, such wishes went perpetually unfulfilled at the North Pole.

My shoulder bones drooped. Six-pack or not, it was nice to disengage from existence for a bit, putting work problems out of my mind and reveling in hours of merriment with Santa. We'd connected on an emotional level—a rarity for immortal guys with disparate roles. He inspired cheer, while I brought on dread. Who knew we'd become good friends, the quintessential odd couple?

The powerful wind gusts blew harder against my skeleton, driving me back as I struggled to push forward. Good thing my tattered cloak offered some wind-resistance.

The snow-covered ground was unstable—I couldn't tell what was level ground and what was a pile of snow. One misstep and I'd find myself neck-bone-deep in snow. Pulling myself out would've been a joy.

When I saw Santa, I'd be sure to give him a handshake, maybe even a hug followed by a slap on the back. I'd express my profound respect for him and eternal loyalty. He'd truly shown what a great guy he was, which blew my mind more than the morning wind. I felt a kinship I'd never known. Maybe it was Christmas magic. Or maybe it was Santa's magnetism.

Santa, a drinker? I threw my skull back, laughing.

I normally didn't consider myself the expressive type, but I felt the urge to open up to him. It wasn't a very reaper thing to do, but I felt the compulsion. Perhaps it was because we're both ancient and have been around long enough to know what was important. I took in a deep, contented breath.

Whether I got the chance to express my feelings or not, choosing to hang out with him showed how important he was to me. Even if I stayed mum, a mere sentence or two said a million unspoken things.

I turned my shoulder inward as the fierce winds battered my bones.

As his house came into view, guilt settled in my abdominal cavity. For a long time, I'd nursed a bitter resentment toward him. I'd harbored unpleasant thoughts about him, thoughts which I dared not entertain now after getting to know his jolly, truly good nature.

I squinted and lowered my brow bones. I didn't want to think about my envy. But the rest of the journey forced me to investigate it.

I'd unfairly compared myself to him, putting him on a pedestal while I groveled in the dirt below. My mistake was buying into the illusion. Truth was, Santa deserved his legendary status. He was the man of the midnight hour, the shooting star of the festive holiday, and the toast of every town around the world. He merited every bit of adoration he received, from young and old. He even earned my adoration—and a reaper didn't give it easily.

I suppose my envy had tried to tell me something: that what Santa had, I wanted. But everything about his life was a front—unreal, a show for the masses.

At the heart of it all, he was just like me.

I drew closer to Santa's house. With a jolt of adrenaline, I crunched through the snow.

He appeared, waving his plump hand. "Ho-ho-ho! Good to see you, pal!"

I waved back and let out a sigh. The world and the afterworld were good places.

"Did you hear, Reaper? A big blizzard is coming our way in two days!"

My eye sockets bulged. I took two steps back, nearly tripping over my snowshoes and falling sitbones first into the snow. A blizzard at the North Pole? In two days?

I did a rapid calculation in my skull. Two days meant December 24th—Christmas Eve!

A nauseating sickness overwhelmed me. As I bowled over grasping my abdominal cavity, the landscape began to whir. I felt I was about to faint. My entire skeleton needed to lean against something stable.

"Are you sure?" I managed to cough out, stumbling in the snow as Santa grabbed my arm bone to support me.

"Yep, the elves warned me. It's in the weather forecast. For the wee morning hours." His gray eyes grew big, and his bushy white brows rose up. "They say it's going be a mean one."

Then it hit me: Death's upcoming blizzard, his deadliest storm yet in the Arctic region. And Santa was on his list!

I pressed my fist against my jawbone.

Being distracted by my fun-filled days with Santa, I'd forgotten all about the deadly blizzard. I'd even neglected to perform my daily habit of checking my client schedule.

My breath grew quick and shallow. Within the minute, I was hyperventilating. I couldn't let my good pal perish amid the upcoming onslaught.

I turned and, with my two hand bones, grabbed Santa by the trim of his velvety red suit. We stood face to face, so close I smelled the sharp menthol on his peppermint breath. Staring like a madcap reaper into his surprised eyes, I demanded, "You have to evacuate."

Laid-back and jolly as ever, Santa shooed me with his hand. "Relax, Reaper. I'm not afraid of a little blizzard. I've lived through countless blizzards in the North Pole, wild as can be, over the last seventeen hundred years." He made expansive gestures with his hands, as if to illustrate the storms' ferocity.

I felt my toe bones go numb. My skeleton began sweating profusely.

"No, you don't understand," I pleaded, still clutching his suit tightly. An overwhelming sensation of dread overcame me. "This blizzard is different. You and the elves have to leave now." My eye sockets grew wide and my jawbone remained parted as I listened for Santa's answer without taking breath.

"Come on, Reaper. Don't be a fool. Blizzards come and go all the time at the top of the world. It's the natural order of things. I plan to ride it out as I always do and protect my home. I'm not leaving." He stood with his hands defiantly on his hips.

With my rib cage caved in, I unclenched my fist bones and let go of his suit. The first frown in four days appeared on my face bones. I couldn't meet his gaze.

"Don't look so disheartened, Reaper," Santa said in soothing tone. "Here, I'll show you how it's done here in the North Pole."

He grasped my tattered cloak and yanked me toward his house. I stumbled along in the snow like an inflatable snowman with no energy or will of its own.

"There, see?" he asked before we reached the front door. He pointed to a steel-encased generator next to the house. "I'm prepared, no matter how cold it gets."

I scowled. A generator was no match for a certain demise.

We took a few more steps through the snow. Shovels lay against the side of the house, near multiple bags of rock salt sat.

Santa dragged me the roundabout way, passing the barn. He poked his head through the massive breezeway door. "And my reindeer have enough hay and water until the storm passes."

I grudgingly peeked inside. The animals certainly did have plenty of nourishment. Humph. A lot good that would do Santa.

He pulled me back toward the front and into his home. Slouching, and with my arm bones hanging limply by my sides, I followed.

We entered his cozy kitchen, where I'd savored that delicious existence-saving meal of freshly baked ham in the company of greatness. I glanced up. Rising to the ceiling was a huge, teetering pile of dozens of boxed mashed potatoes, packaged fruitcakes, and canned cranberry sauce.

"Don't say I don't have enough good eats." He grabbed his big belly, which shook like strawberry Jell-O. "Ho-ho-ho!"

My facial features went slack.

In the corner of the kitchen stood stacks upon stacks of water bottles shrink wrapped in plastic. "My water supply is pretty impressive," he said. "Wouldn't you say?"

I couldn't bring myself to answer a question about something that wouldn't save him.

"See all those pots? They'll allow me to melt snow and boil water."

Sighing long, my shoulder bones drooped even further.

"Oh, and my stash of beer will keep me warm during the cold blizzard."

A drink right now wouldn't do me any good, only amplify my intense concern. I knitted my brow bones as he dragged me into the living room, furnished with a cushiony couch, a chestnut coffee table, and multiple portable heaters.

"I'll stay toasty inside," he said, as I stared blankly at the heaters. "No storm blowing minus forty-degree winds will put me out of commission," he said, laughing as if the upcoming blizzard were nothing but a mere powder dusting.

What did Santa know? My empty insides felt unbearably heavy.

"Now, don't you think I forgot about my daily essentials. I've got all the toothpaste and shampoo I need to take care of my smile and my famous white locks." He stroked his long beard. "A man in my position doesn't need too many shaving supplies, though. A simple beard trimmer keeps things tidy."

I wished to escape the throes of my harsh reality and into my imagination. At least there I'd whisk Santa away to safety, preventing his upcoming demise.

He sat on the heavily used couch and motioned for me to sit on the equally worn recliner across. I plodded over the red vintage rug and dropped into the seat with a heavy sigh. He pulled out a yellowed slip of paper from his pants pocket. "Let's see. Flashlight, check. Batteries, check."

Still holding the list, he glanced up at me. "You know, I've even got a deicer spray for the front door lock just in case it freezes. No blizzard will trap Santa inside on

Christmas Eve!" He laughed heartily.

I felt hollowed out, though I literally was. Clearly, he didn't see the severity of the situation. I dropped my chin bone into my hand bone, which rested on my knee bone.

He inched to the edge of the couch. "Don't look so glum, Reaper. Christmas will go on as it always does. Nothing will stop it." He cleared his throat. "I'll give you a tip. Petroleum jelly. It's a saving grace during blizzard conditions. I slathered a thick layer onto the hinges of my sleigh this morning, just so I'm able to open the door, hop in, and deliver presents like I'm supposed to—even in the midst of a brutal storm." He gave me a wink.

I sat immersed in a sludge of self-hatred.

"If it makes you feel any better, I stay in close contact with my trusty elves," he said with his charming rosy Santa smile. "They send me alerts and updates on the nasty weather conditions. Oh, and one of my elves is a decent plumber. If my water pipes burst, he'll fix it before you can say Rudolph. If you ever need a good plumber, just ask. I'd be happy to connect you with him."

"Gee, thanks, Santa." I dropped my gaze and stared listlessly at my lap.

"Not even hypothermia will get to me," he boasted. "I'm aware of all the signs: purplish skin, numbness, and tingling." He leaned in toward me and, his gray eyes sparkling, whispered, "Remember, we're immortals. The things we have to face nevertheless." He threw his arms and head back, laughing.

Immortals, yeah. Until Death made his fateful mistake.

"The home's fortified," Santa added, "complete with a winterized roof. Holes are no good up there." He pointed his plump index finger to the ceiling. "Chimney's clean so I can relax beside a crackling fire when the blizzard whips like a maniac outside."

I glanced at the cuckoo clock on the wall. The bird hadn't chirped all day. Time seemed to slow down—but not enough to stop the blizzard on the twenty-fourth from causing doom to one and all here at the lonely, desolate top of the world.

With a happy grunt, Santa hoisted himself up from the couch. "Speaking of winterizing, why don't you lend me a hand with the weatherstripping? Need to add a few extra pieces to the front door and windows. Seal them up real good."

Overcome with poignant emotion my voice cracked. "Uh, sure."

Sighing, I got up and began helping him with the cumbersome rolls.

"Less is more!" he said, referring to the adhesive. I blindly followed his installation instructions.

As we glued the weatherstripping to the door, Santa said in a jolly tone, "If anything, the spirit of Christmas will keep me warm and safe."

Choking up, I kept mum.

I finished helping Santa install the extra weatherstripping. It was a necessary task, especially since he was staying put in the upcoming blizzard despite my protests. Still, I needed a good excuse to leave. I saw the strong urge to flee to headquarters to right this egregious wrong.

"Listen, Santa," I said, biting my jawbone. "As much as I'd like to spread the holiday cheer, I can't hang out the rest of the day. I've got urgent work to do. Duty calls."

Immediately, my mind envisioned the worst-case scenario. He'd be offended, or worse, feel excruciatingly lonely in the days leading up to Christmas. He might've even felt rejected—something I knew all too well. I didn't want him experiencing distress, self-doubt, or any other emotional nonsense.

"Oh-oh, I completely understand, Reaper. I know what it's like to be so needed at work."

I flung my skull back. He commiserated with me, proving again the admirable extent of his congeniality.

Then he sent me off with a friendly wave and a rosy smile that lit up my eye sockets.

With a furrowed brow bone and an alert gaze, I raced like a spirited thoroughbred across the endless cosmos, back to headquarters. Prudently, I'd chosen not to take the scenic route as I had while traveling to the North Pole. Fun as it had been, time was of the essence now. The blizzard was scheduled in two days, and I needed to protect Santa from a horrible doom.

The only way to stop the blizzard from taking Santa's life was to persuade Death to correct his drunken mistake. It'd take no more than a minute or two for him to review the schedule, realize his blunder, then quickly delete the time and date of death—returning Santa to his immortal state again.

Even if the blizzard swept across the North Pole and covered the landscape in a frightening deluge of snow, wind, and ice, no one would be hurt. Not the elves and especially not my twin flame Santa. That was Death's awesome power.

A few clicks on the spreadsheet, and the jolly old man would be saved forever.

I swung open the front door to the building and hurried inside. Panting heavily, I scrambled up the stairs decked with holly. I reached the second floor and, brushing aside the glittery blue snowflake ceiling streamers, stormed toward Death's office.

Trying to exude calm and focus, I was intent on making my case to the big boss. This mistake would be corrected at this very instant, if I could help it.

But I stopped dead in my tracks. The boss's door was closed. The lights weren't on. I looked around, swallowing excessively.

Normally, Death kept his office door ajar, an intentional sign of his open-door policy and openness to hearing employee feedback. He always strived to make the afterworld a better place for everyone. That's what made it a joy to work for him.

Maybe he was taking a nap and wanted peace and quiet. The office team could get boisterous during the merry holidays.

Grunting, I jiggled the doorknob. But it didn't turn. Humph.

Frantic, I spun around. Maybe Life would have answers. I rushed to her door but it, too, was shut and locked. I grabbed my skull, not knowing what to do.

Then, as holiday jingles played from the speakers, my ear bones picked up the jovial sounds of singing near the back conference room. I sprinted for the raucous.

Larry strode out with a cup of hot cocoa. "Reaper! You're just in time."

My eye sockets widened. "For what?"

"The team's singing carol karaoke. Some of us are even performing parody lyrics." His brown eyebrows bobbed up and down.

The spirit guide tugged me by the sleeve of my cloak.

"Come on, join us!"

I recoiled.

"Ah, don't be self-conscious. It's not like we're singing pop songs. It's only Christmas carols. You know all the words. We hear them played every hour from the office speakers."

Oh boy, did I hear them. Every. Single. Hour.

"Look, Larry. I need to speak to Death. It's important. He's not in his office. Neither is Life." I spoke with an unwavering firmness in my voice. I wasn't dilly dallying—not to sing holiday carols, not to make merry under the ceiling of Christmas baubles, not to join the staff in their spirit of togetherness. My one task was to save my good pal from an awful, untimely demise.

"Death? Oh, he's on vacay with Life in the Bahamas."

"Bahamas?"

"Yeah, the weather is sublime this time of year. They're probably drinking White Christmas Mojitos while lounging by the beach next to the warm turquoise water."

My finger bones touched my parted jawbone.

Larry looked off dreamily. "I bet they're dining on fresh caught fish, crab salad, baked macaroni and cheese, and oven roasted turkey right now."

The spirit guide licked his lips.

"Life mentioned she and Death would be up at exactly two a.m. to watch the colorful Junkanoo dancing on Christmas Day," he said.

"What's a Junkanoo?" I asked, scratching my temple.

"It's the Bahamian Christmas masquerade," he explained, taking a sip of his hot cocoa. "I hear it's a spirited celebration of dancing and music, with lots of beating drums and whistles."

"Thanks, Larry. I'll see ya." I touched his elbow briefly and turned to go.

"What about caroling?" he yelled as I sped off.

I had to get to the Bahamas and find Death. But the Bahamas, more than anywhere else on Earth, was a prime destination for lovers of sand and sun, especially during the Christmas season. I'd have a hard time spotting Death lounging on the crowded beaches, snorkeling in the water, swimming with the native sharks, or getting friendly with the stingrays. Though Death was larger than life, it'd take a keen eye to find him or anyone else on the island during its busiest part of the year.

With the blizzard scheduled, I didn't have the luxury of time. My other option was to return to the North Pole to try and convince Santa, for the second time, that this blizzard was no meager flurry, and that he needed to evacuate pronto. He, however, seemed to take immense pride in having survived numerous catastrophic blizzards over the ages.

Ugh, the last thing I wanted to do was squash his pride like a stuffed festive, well, squash.

I collapsed into my seat at my desk and dropped my chin bone into my hand bone. What was I to do? It was crucial that I made the right choice. Time wasn't on my side. I didn't have days to persuade Santa to prioritize his own safety.

A gnawing pain grew in the back of my throat bones. I'd accepted the blame in not warning him sooner. I'd been too distracted by all the good times we spent together.

It might've taken longer to try to find Death in the Bahamas. He could've been on any one of its seven hundred islands. Even if I got lucky and spotted him right away, it'd still take time to correct things. He'd have to grudgingly break from his vacation, change out of his swim trunks, return to the office dressed a tad more professionally, then be prepared to make the authorized amendment as quick as possible.

He couldn't simply update my list from the beach, as if he were ordering a cocktail from his smartphone. Each individual expiry took laborious time to schedule and finalize. Any corrections, even last-minute ones, had to be done at headquarters—making it official.

I tilted my skull in a side-to-side rhythm, evaluating each option with careful deliberation. What a tough choice. Only the right decision would prevent the world's most unwarranted passing.

Tapping my index finger bone against my jawbone, I struggled to decide.

Maybe I should flip a coin. I checked my cloak pockets. I didn't have a dime on me. Figures, I was a broke reaper. I tossed out that idea, sank deeper into my seat, and let out a loud exhale.

The second-hand on the round clock steadily ticked away.

I was losing valuable minutes.

I got up and paced around my cubicle with my hand bones clasped behind my backbone, weighing my options.

Refusing to waste any more time, I made my decision.

I'd take the risk and head back to the North Pole and try to convince Santa. Even though he'd refused to budge, I had a better shot at success than trying to locate Death. At least I knew where to find Santa. The man in red wasn't lounging on some crowded beach in the Bahamas during peak tourist season.

But even that was chancy—I might not persuade Santa.

I wrung my hand bones.

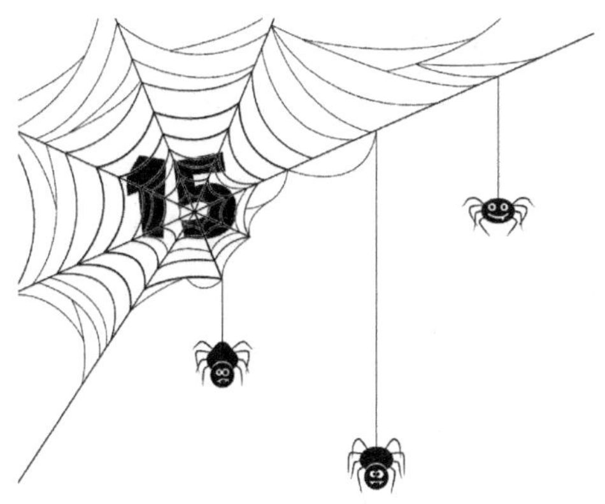

Not wasting another second, I scrambled back to the North Pole—this time through the ethereal cosmos, as opposed to taking the longer, more adventurous land route. It was the morning of the 23rd. I had less than sixteen hours before the epic blizzard devastated the area one minute after midnight.

Moseying around Santa's property, I heard his jolly voice coming from the barn. I stomped through the snow, poked my head through the door, and found him feeding his reindeer.

"Rudolph, now you listen here, old boy," he said, raising the hay bale to feed the animal. "Make sure your red nose is as bright as can be on Christmas Eve. They say a horrible blizzard will be upon us. We want to make sure visibility is good so we can deliver the presents." He patted the reindeer's head.

I rapped on the barn door and right away hunched. What was I doing? Santa was on the brink of a horrible death, and I was being awfully polite by knocking first?

I altered course. With my shoulder bones back, I charged across the dirt ground toward Santa.

He turned, and his rosy face brightened. "Ho-ho-ho, Reaper! Good to see you, friend. Work finished up so fast?"

"Eh, not quite. I'll be busy up to my neck bones in one day's time, if things don't get sorted today."

Seeing no point in making further small talk, I marched up to Santa. It was now or never, win or bust, death or glory. I'd either convince him to leave the North Pole or see my good friend perish before my eye sockets. I didn't fancy carrying a heaviness in my rib cage forever.

I met his gaze directly as he stood there, dressed in an old, yellowed shirt and red fleece pants held up by his snappy red suspenders.

"Listen, Santa—"

He held a palm up to my face bones. "Now, Reaper, don't go trying to persuade me to leave my home. I've been here for ages. I know what blizzards are all about. I'm not going anywhere. Not in tomorrow's blizzard, or any blizzard that threatens me or my livelihood even centuries down the road."

My empty insides shrunk. "You might not get a chance to see another blizzard if you don't save yourself from this one. Do you remember the Great Blizzard of 1888?"

"Oh, yes, very much so, the world's most savage blizzard." Santa shivered, hugging himself. "It was a fierce one. Fifty-eight feet of snow."

I pressed my jawbone together and clenched my fist. "This blizzard promises to be ten times worse. If you stay here tonight, you'll be buried under twice as much snow." I pulled out my phone and showed him a map. "See?" I pointed. "The blizzard is expected to strike down here and then–"

Unfazed, Santa pushed the phone away. "I'm familiar with the North Pole. I've lived here for centuries. I know every ridge, every basin like the back of my hand."

"Santa, if you stay, your entire house and barn and workshop will be buried under a hundred feet of snow. You'd never boil snow fast enough to escape and deliver Christmas gifts on schedule."

He rubbed his white beard and looked off into the distance.

"You must evacuate," I said. "If not for yourself, then for Rudolph, Dancer, Dasher, Prancer, Vixen, Comet, Cupid, Donner, and Blitzen–and your hundreds of thousands of elves."

I looked at him imploringly. It was out of my hand bones–the ball was in his court. His soft gaze had drifted to the corners, as if he were deliberating carefully. I fiddled with the torn edges of my cloak and rubbed my sweaty hand bones on its folds.

After what seemed like eons of gut-wrenching silence, he returned his attention back to me. “I consider myself to be a wise old man,” he started, in a calm, patient tone. “It’s how I’ve survived all these centuries.”

Still unruffled, Santa showed an admirable fearlessness in the face of stark adversity.

“But I hear an earnestness in your voice, Reaper, so I’m going to listen. Plus, you’re my friend. If you say I should evacuate, by golly, I’m going to evacuate.”

I clutched my fist bones to my rib cage and, letting out a squeal, nearly jumped to the roof of the barn.

“Slow your horses, Reaper,” he said.

I tried to follow his example and remain calm. But my excitement got the best of me, and I couldn’t stand still. I wanted to grab him by the hand and set off to safer pastures.

“Where should we go?” he asked, as I bounced on my toe bones.

“Anywhere, as long as it’s far from the North Pole,” I replied with a thousand-watt grin.

He scratched his chin. “How ‘bout Australia? I know it’s warm this time of year.”

“Or all year, but that’s no matter.” I grabbed his hand and held it. A feeling of sheer joy swelled in my rib cage. “You made the right decision, Santa. I promise you.”

“That’s all well and good, but I need to inform my elves about the new evacuation plan.”

"Oh, yes, sir. I'll get out of your way." I stepped aside as he left the barn and made arrangements to instruct his elves to leave the North Pole today.

A few hours later, as I played with the reindeer in the barn, Santa informed me his elves were building thousands of light aircraft.

"They're quite the speedy workers," he said, "having hands-on experience building all sorts of vehicles to give as Christmas gifts. Classic cars, sports, cars, even exotic cars. Building miniature planes with plenty of cargo space to store the Christmas presents is right up their alley." He laughed merrily. "They should be finished before dinner."

"Great." I bounced from foot bone to foot bone.

"The reindeer have been fed, so they're energized and prepared to fly. Now all I need to do is add a layer of coating to my sleigh. It'll reduce the drag as I fly and make my journey smoother." He waddled outside and to his sleigh.

A light snow had covered the red contraption. He brushed it off with a bristled snow brush. Then, crouching, he opened a bottle of ceramic coating, poured a generous dollop onto his rag, and began applying it in circular motions to the sides, front, and rear.

It took him a couple hours to coat the entire sleigh, front to back. By then, the elves had completed their task of building enough miniature planes to fly themselves out of the North Pole and to Australia's eight-thousand warm islands.

"Right on time," Santa said, looking at his wristwatch. "They'll be flying off a few elves per plane with the gifts stashed in the cargo areas."

"Excellent." Things were moving as planned.

The icy wind picked up. Gusts blew a flurry of snow nonstop, creating whiteout conditions. I could no longer see the majestic holiday tree in Santa's front yard. The temperature plummeted to below fifty degrees, turning my toe and finger bones into icicles.

It was six o'clock in the evening. I looked up at the darkened sky, looming ominously over us. The snow clouds had blocked the northern lights, preventing me from seeing their comforting glow.

I shivered. "You better get going."

"Right, right." He calmly hitched up his reindeer and took his seat in the sleigh.

He leaned to his right, over the side door, and looked at the front of the sleigh. "Something's off," he said. "One corner is sitting unusually low."

"Just go." I trembled as the portent of doom rumbled through the night sky.

Santa sighed. His busy white brows grew closer. "I don't know about this. I'll give it a test run."

He yanked the reins lightly, and the reindeer pranced forward slowly like nimble dancers.

I wiped my hand bone over my forehead bone, relieved Santa was on his way to safety.

But instantly, the sleigh started pulling to one side.

"Whoa!" he yelled.

The reindeer, obedient to their jolly master, stopped in their tracks.

"What's the matter?" I asked, breaking out in a cold sweat.

"I don't know." He got out and began inspecting the sleigh.

A restlessness came on. My bones grew twitchy.

"Got it," he said pointing under the sleigh. "The suspension's collapsed."

"What?" My eye sockets widened. A broken sleigh was bad news!

"I can't drive like this," he said. "The sleigh will pull dangerously to one side. It'll drift and pull during turns, putting my reindeers' lives at risk. And the noise is terrible!"

My posture crumpled. He was so close to saving himself. I shook my skull in denial, then glanced at my smartwatch. Eight o'clock. Four hours and one minute till the deadly blizzard flattened the entire North Pole like a gingerbread pancake.

The wind lashed, billowing icy snowflakes in every direction. Visibility lessened. I was inside a snow globe, shaken up by some malicious entity.

"You've got to fix it!" I yelled through the whipping wind.

"I'll need my elves, whoever's still here, to build me premium shocks. It'll help with ride control. Otherwise..." He made a dropping gesture with his hands.

"No, we don't want you crashing to the ground just before Christmas," I said, choking up.

Santa trudged through the blowing snow to his house to contact the remaining elves who hadn't yet flown off to warmer climes. Moments later, he returned with a wrench, a ball joint puller kit, and a spring compressor. Kneeling on the heavy wet snow, he began fixing his sleigh.

I paced back and forth, as Santa patiently began replacing the broken springs, ball joints, strut mounts, and tie rod ends. He remained serene, as I muttered to myself like a reaper on the verge of madness.

I checked the time again. Ten o'clock—two hours, one minute before the moment of doom.

The darkness grew intense, and the wind howled colder, shriller, like a hungry beast chasing its long-stalked prey.

My teeth chattered. My breathing grew quicker. A nausea overcame me. Was this the last I'd see of my pal, Santa Claus?

Minutes later, I stood next to the sleigh hyperventilating, barely able to think straight enough to count the seconds to one minute past midnight. Time raced at lightning speed, filling me with a horrible, mounting dread. In fact, Santa *was* in a race against time.

I clenched and unclenched my fist bones, every now and then letting out an involuntary whimper—a very reaper thing to do. A few beers would've soothed my hysterics right about now.

The chilly wind whiplashed in every direction, hurling blinding snow. I felt as if I were being smothered in the increasingly heavier, whipping snowfall. I kept repeating to myself that things would turn out okay, even though I didn't believe myself. Only the worst-case scenario played on repeat in my mind, tormenting me. If only I'd warned Santa sooner, he wouldn't be in this hot mess on this frigid night.

Santa manipulated his tools in the barren cold, crouching in the snow and focusing his attention underneath the sled.

Out of nowhere, a huge whoosh dropped snow on us. My jaw went dry. My ear bones rang. This was it. This was the moment of doom. I steeled myself for a second death—and Santa's first.

But he calmly shook off the snow, never took his eyes off the sleigh, and kept working.

A *click* sounded. I whipped my skull around, hyper-reactive to the slightest indication that the end of everything was near.

"That should do it," Santa said, leaning back.

"What? Fixed?"

"Yep, sleigh's all fixed." He hoisted himself up.

I looked upward, thanking my lucky stars.

"That's great! You best get a move on," I cried out, the puff of my breath freezing into ice crystals.

"Yeah, the wind's picking up." Santa hopped into his sleigh and grabbed the reins. "Hike!" The reindeer started to prance, then lifted the sleigh into the air.

Before I knew it, Santa was airborne.

"Keep me updated!" I yelled to him, waving.

"I will!" he shouted back from a thousand feet up in the frosty air.

I watched Santa, his sleigh, and his nine reindeer fly through the night sky. Even though visibility had grown to zero in the pre-blizzard conditions, their silhouettes somehow stood out against the full moon. Such was the power of Christmas magic.

I let out a huge exhale and wiped my forehead bone. Santa had escaped in the nick of time.

Speaking of time, it was wise for me to leave too. Otherwise, I'd be buried under a hundred of feet of snow—a horrible second death. I made a hasty exit out of the North Pole.

With no particular place to go on Christmas Eve Eve, I returned to headquarters. The office was open year-round—as matters of life, death, and the afterlife never stopped rolling.

The grassy park surrounding the building looked inviting, so I took a stroll. The weather felt cool, but not as unforgettably icy as the North Pole at this time of year.

My attention was drawn to a wooden bench at the edge of the sidewalk—the perfect place to take a much-needed nap. After all the stress and commotion of trying to evacuate Santa, I needed a nice, peaceful rest. I laid my skeleton flat on the bench and covered myself with the extra folds of my cloak.

I didn't know how many hours had passed when I was awoken by a chirp from my phone.

Lying on the bench, slightly disoriented from exhaustion, I pulled the device out of my pocket.

"Reaper!" said a familiar, cheery voice.

Santa's rosy face appeared on my screen. He'd started a video chat with me in real time.

I bolted upright, my eye sockets glued to my phone.

"Santa!"

"I made it Reaper. Here I am on Australia's sunny Kangaroo Island." His face and tone expressed joy and well-being. And why wouldn't he be happy? He'd landed on the pristine beaches of the Land Down Under.

He rotated his device to show me the grassy lands next to the endless stretches of beaches, the sunlit sky, and the swirling blue water behind him.

"Maryanna, who knew better, texted while driving. The tablet I'm using was intended for her on Christmas. But because of her recklessness, she made it on my Naughty list. And now it's mine."

I threw my skull back and laughed.

"Oh, and the elves landed safely on the islands of Bathurst, Flinders, and K'gari," he said. "But here on Kangaroo Island, I'm surrounded by clean air, the music of birdsongs, and lots of kangaroos with joeys in their pouches hopping around. Koala bears are lounging in the trees, nibbling on leaves."

In the background, kangaroos with brown fur coats hopped across the tall, untamed grass and sparred playfully with each other like amateur boxers in a ring.

"What an awesome place to land," I said.

"Awesome, indeed. It's a magical place—just the spot for someone as magical as me. I feel a sense of healing here amid untouched nature, especially after having barely escaped the harrowing blizzard."

I noticed Rudolph grazing leisurely in the grass behind him.

"I let my reindeer loose, and they're blending right in with the kangaroos." He laughed merrily. "Well, I just wanted to let you know we're all safe. Now, I've got some Christmas presents to deliver. I'll start out by flying east to deliver gifts to everyone in the Republic of Kiribati who made it on my Nice list.

"Kiribati?" I asked, having nearly forgotten about that tiny island near Fiji. I hadn't picked up souls there in a long time, because hardly anyone died.

"Yeah, the youthful island nation in the Pacific dotted with coconut palms. I go there every Christmas to deliver gifts. It's usually my first stop, because it's got the earliest time zone in the world. After that, I make my way westward to deliver gifts to the rest of humanity."

My skeleton relaxed.

"Anyway, duty calls. I've got to go. I don't want to be video chatting and driving the sleigh. It's distracting and unsafe—which is a no-no." He waved his index finger back and forth. "I don't want to be on my own Naughty list."

"All right. I'll be seeing ya," I told him in a bubbly tone.

He ended the chat and, sighing, I tucked my phone back into my pocket.

I sat for a moment to reflect before heading to the office. A warmth filled my empty insides, knowing my friend would live to see another Christmas, and infinite Christmases more. That the world would still have Santa.

I sauntered up the decked stairs, noticing for the first time how lovely the red bows looked and how breathtakingly beautiful the string of green, red, and purple lights glowed, almost like the Northern Lights captured in teensy bulbs. Along the way to my desk, the holiday music playing through the speakers sounded gleeful to my ear bones. I never knew it could be so uplifting.

As I sat down, I glanced at the weather report on my phone. The blizzard had occurred right on schedule, precisely at 12:01 a.m., burying the North Pole under one hundred feet of snow. Per the news report, no one was expected to survive.

I leaned back in my chair, clasping my hand bones behind my skull. I'd saved my good friend. Phew. I'd also saved myself months of hard work picking up hundreds of thousands of elf souls who'd otherwise have been swept under the deluge of Arctic blizzard snow.

A smile spread across my face bones. Come to think of it, I'd just saved *Christmas*.

On Christmas Day, having no one with whom to sit by a warm fire or pull apart a circle of gooey Monkey Bread, I hung out at the office. It was pretty empty, with everyone spending time with their loved ones.

I walked to my desk, along the way glancing at all the staff's photo frames on their desk. The displays of affection between my bubbly colleagues and their near-and-dears gave me a bittersweet feeling.

As I sat at my desk, the heavy silence around me grew oppressive. Nothing was happening in the office, no holiday caroling, no bustling hot cocoa station, not even an ugly sweater station to run from. Yet stress overwhelmed me, and the festering feeling refused to go away.

I decided to distract myself with work. I turned on my computer and began drafting a long email to Death, explaining what had just transpired regarding Santa. I ended it with a suggestion to add a system of checks to prevent future immortals from perishing under erroneous circumstances.

I hit Send. The boss would read my email when he returned on the 26th, and everything would be settled.

I sat back in my chair and sighed. A hollowness overwhelmed me, despite being literally empty inside. With no one around, not even good ol' Larry or any of the other spirit guides, the sense of isolation tormented me to the bone.

I looked at the red and green baubles hanging from the ceiling. The entire world celebrated in the spirit of togetherness, while I moped around at the office without another entity in sight. At least I had my memories of Santa and our adventures.

As I remembered him fondly, happy tears welled up in my eye sockets. I cocked my skull to the side as the memories took over. Feeling relaxed, I forgot my loneliness for a splendid moment.

Rather than wallow in self-pity here, I decided to go back to my rental. At least I could light up the fireplace and feel toasty by the snapping flames—even if alone.

Tucking my hand bones in my cloak pockets, my skull hung low, I made the trip back home. At least it wasn't perpetually dark, like the North Pole this time of year. Despite the overcast skies, the sun peeked through the clouds. The daylight gave me a little pep, and I kicked random pebbles.

As I lumbered down the empty streets, my phone chirped. My pulse raced. Who'd be thinking of me on Christmas Day?

I wasted no time yanking out my phone.

"Ho-ho-ho, merry Christmas, Reaper!" Santa said, chipper as can be.

It was my dear old buddy on his special day wishing me a joyous one! A welcome rush of happiness filled every vacant space between my bones.

"Santa, merry Christmas to you too," I gushed back with an ear bone-to-ear bone grin.

"I'm still here in Australia soaking up the sun. I finished delivering all the presents a few hours ago, took a nap, and now I'm ready to hit the water. I'm going surfing!"

"That's neat, Santa," I said, as a bouncy walk replaced my lumbering one.

"Yep, I'm using my brand-new waterproof action camera to take shots of me riding the waves." His rosy cheeks looked even rosier under the sunlight in comparison to the darkness of the North Pole. I saw his every laugh line as he smiled, and he had many more than I'd initially thought.

"A gift intended for another person who made it on your Naughty list?" I asked, referring to his camera.

"Yep, naughty at the last minute still means naughty. Now this dandy little thing is mine," he said, throwing his head back laughing.

Holding his action camera, he hopped onto a surfboard wearing his Santa hat and a pair of red shorts, then paddled out on his belly toward the waves, his one arm still taking the video.

I was impressed. I never knew Santa could surf. But he was in the Land Down Under, and that's what Aussies did on Christmas Day.

He hopped onto the surfboard and caught a magnificent wave. "Ho-ho-ho!" he yelled, laughing, and clearly having a grand time.

The wow factor of Santa in shorts catching a wave imprinted on my mind. My admiration for him grew a hundred times greater—even at sixty, he lived to the fullest!

A few waves later, he returned to the beach.

"Gotta hand it to you, Santa," I said, watching him in real time. "You know how to ride a wave."

"Yep, gifted many a surfboard in my time. Surfing's energizing, even relaxing, after making all those Christmas Eve deliveries. But I need a break from it."

Back on the beach, he threw on a green t-shirt with a holiday tree printed on front and red snowflake flipflops. "I'm on my way to the local markets to do a prawn run. Then I'll make myself a nice Christmas lunch. Wish you were here, Reaper. I'm having the time of my life."

"I wish I was there too, Santa." I wiped away a happy tear.

"Well, I'll catch you later. We'll hang out again soon. Bye-bye!" He gave me a smile and a friendly wave.

I tucked my phone back into my cloak pocket. Closing my eye sockets, I tipped my skull back.

What a guy. He made me feel like I counted on Christmas Day. He filled that gaping hole in my rib cage with something nice. I drank in the moment, not planning on letting that feeling go.

With a hop in my step, I skip-danced all the way back to my rental in jolly reaper style.

I kindled a fire in my fireplace, pushing the logs back and forth until a crackling fire blazed. The warmth felt good against the bottoms of my cold feet bones as I stretched my skeleton out before the fireplace. Trying to get comfy, I turned, only to notice an unfamiliar box underneath my spindly, bare holiday tree.

My jawbone parted. I stared at the box for a good moment, my brow bones raised. Curiosity got the best of me, and I scrambled toward it.

As I turned the box over examining it, my breath hitched. It was a present, all wrapped up in shiny blue paper with a shimmery white bow on top! Who'd think of me this time of year?

The box felt heavy in my hand bones. Something, perhaps marvelous, lay inside. Only one way to find out. Carefully, I began peeling the wrapping paper away. With my finger bones touching my parted jawbone, I gasped. It was a Christmas gift, the first I'd ever received. I gathered the wrapping paper, which I'd cherish forever—and as an eternal reaper, I meant *forever*.

The beginnings of a sleek black box came into view. I opened it—and yelped. Inside was a luxurious wooden bracket tray, whiskey stones, and wood chips in four flavors: walnut, oak, cherry, and apple. Along with these came an oak smoker, tongs, a spoon and—a butane torch.

I let out a bark of laughter as my jawbone dropped to the floor. Good golly! A cocktail smoker kit *with* a torch.

Letting out a loud whoop, I thrust my fist bones into the air and did a jig.

But who in the afterworld could this be from? Searching the wrapping paper for a card, I found it taped to one side. It read *From Santa*.

I pressed my hand bones against my rib cage and nodded.

Santa had gotten my letter, after all. Christmas magic—was real. A celebration was in store!

I reached to the mantel top for a half-filled liquor bottle, quickly grabbed a glass, and poured myself a whiskey. I felt my unbreakable brofriendship with Santa at this very moment.

I dropped in the whiskey stones to chill my drink. Capping the glass with the smoker top, I filled it with the oak woodchips I fancied, then ignited them with the torch's thin blue flame. The smoke wafted down into the glass in beautiful ethereal wisps, infusing my whiskey with just the right level of bold, jawbone-smacking flavor. I held up the clear glass, admiring my cocktail from all sides.

I raised my drink. Here's to my bro, Santa.

Leaning back, I savored the smokiest whiskey I'd ever had, on the most joyous Christmas Day.

Other books in the Grim Reaper Adventure series

A Morbid Obsession: A Grim Reaper Comedy Adventure

Crossing Over and Back: A Grim Reaper Comedy Adventure

Thank you for reading *A Holly Jolly Reaper: A Grim Reaper Holiday Adventure.* Please leave a review if you enjoyed this holiday tale!

www.riyapresents.com

www.ingramcontent.com/pod-product-compliance
Lightning Source LLC
Chambersburg PA
CBHW071944190726
48293CB00004B/1343

* 9 7 8 1 9 5 6 4 9 6 5 3 6 *